CANTOS OF ARCADIA

NICHOLAS KOTAR

PRESS

ALSO BY NICHOLAS KOTAR

The Raven Son Series:

The Song of the Sirin

The Curse of the Raven

The Heart of the World

The Forge of the Covenant

The Throne of the Gods

The Worldbuilding Series:

How to Survive a Russian Fairy Tale

Heroes for All Times

A Window to the Russian Soul

Russian Fairy Tales and Myths:

In a Certain Kingdom: Fairy Tales of Old Russia

In a Certain Kingdom: Epic Tales of the Rus

In a Certain Land: Wise Fools, Cunning Dragons, and Baba Yaga

Children of Vasyllia:

The Son of the Deathless

To Benedict, for all the beautiful years

CANTO I

"Imperishable [corrupted], thy right arm controls the course of human life. I give thee thanks for all thy benefits, those known and those hidden from me...

...I was born in this world a weak, defenseless child, but thy ... [corrupted] ... his bright wings over my cradle to defend me. From then on thy love hath illumined my path, wondrously guiding me; from birth until now ... [corrupted] showered upon me. I give thanks together with all who have come to know thee, who call upon thy name:

Glory to thee for calling me to life.

Glory to thee, showing me the beauty of the universe."

(FRAGMENTS *from the personal notebook of Ansel Horowitz, final priest of the Ghost Dance)*

WHEN ASKED about it in his later years, Ansel Horowitz claimed to have no memory of the morning that he saved the world.

It could have been a typical enough morning, which at that time of his late 40's would have meant an automated tap on a sawari gong nudging him toward wakefulness. That sound would have been followed by a flicker in the Art Nouveau-inspired LED fixtures waxing from reddish to golden light. His diffuser would have clicked from a night-scent of orange and bergamot to sandalwood, which he always associated with a good, proper shave. A fifteen-minute meditation in bed later, he'd be aware enough to lift a single leg over the edge of his floor-level futon to let his bare feet rasp against the stone floor. The energy of the earth's core—not that far underneath his bedroom—thrummed right up his leg.

That cold thrill led him into musings about the nature of time and to consider that really there were no mornings in the deep caverns of the Ghost Dance Military Energy Installation (GDMEI, or as the idiots called it, "G'day mate"). There were no nights, either. There were times of respite from the darkness, and there was the darkness.

What else would there be? They were buried deep in the earth, right along the Ghost Dance crustal fault near Yucca Mountain in New Mexico. A deep tunnel network, organized into emplacement corridors. Or tombs, if you like, of the unsteady, radiating dead—uranium pellets encased in iron and copper, left under the earth to eke out their half-lives for millennia. The excrement of a dark age.

Such thoughts, he had learned after year five in Ghost Dance, were not to be judged, but simply set aside.

Easier said than done, of course. All the trimmings of Ansel Horowitz might suggest a Western neo-Buddhist of the more enlightened kind. Had anyone actually called Ansel that to his face, he would have smiled blandly at them, while inside, something nasty would be grinning maniacally.

Then again, that morning could have been one of a number of less gentle mornings. He could have, for example, woken up in terror from the drowning dreams. He could have had tech hallucinations—half dream, half afterglow from the substrate musings seeping through his implant. Those dreaming visions often ended with the earth itself blowing up in a cloud of firework sparks.

Whichever type of morning it was, what followed waking had the precision required of all Ghost Dancers (if they wanted to keep their sanity, that is):

1. Shower in naturally heated water smelling faintly of sulfur.

2. Put on previously prepped corduroy pants and button up shirt (powder blue or pink, depending on mood).

3. Line up buttons of shirt exactly to belt buckle.

4. Breathe deeply three times, reaching hands up to the ceiling, brushing it with the tip of the middle finger of the right hand.

5. Put on work jacket, invariably herringbone or tweed.

6. Call in breakfast order to be ready in the canteen: two eggs over easy with turkey bacon (vat grown, unfortunately).

7. Start work.

That fateful day, the call came a number of hours into the first time block. At first, Ansel Horowitz paid no attention. Or no more than to grunt into his nose, a sound that his interns would have recognized as an unconscious delegation mechanism. His mind was busy fashioning complex mathematical models, like filigreed geometric lattices, in the virtual subspace he shared as the human counterpart in the engineer-processor centaur. The implant in his temple thrummed in concert with the one in his heart in a way that suggested that the Ghost, his AI counterpart, had accepted the model and was already refining the structures in ways Ansel couldn't begin to imagine.

Making them fitting for inhabitation.

Ansel's great hope. To see the Ghost in a form of his own choosing. Or would the Ghost perhaps choose a female form? He tried to convince himself that it didn't matter. That the Ghost was a tool, not a person.

Not yet *a person...*

There it was again, Ansel's secret hope. That the AI would make the jump to sentience. That, in spite of everyone using the Ghost for their own needs and (sometimes) lurid desires, it would still turn to him in recognition and say the one thing Ansel wanted to hear more than anything in the world:

"Hello, Father..."

The phone call, again. It was a dial tone that some hack electrician probably thought was funny, with its hint of the dark age of smartphones. But then it struck Ansel Horowitz: no one ever called Ghost Dance. Phones didn't work in the emplacement corridors.

He didn't even *have* a phone. Hardly anyone who was

anyone did, anymore. No need, not with universal incorporation into the subspace.

The magic shattered, the lattices melted, and his implants fell still.

He wanted to scream. But Ansel Horowitz was a man who put much stock in the self-control that comes with a rooted sense of the past. The perfect row of black fountain pens with tortoise-shell handles on the right side of his mahogany desk should be ample proof of that. Just the fact that he even *had* pens on his desk should be proof of that! And the immaculately dusted subspace interface—it still looked so much like those museum-grade Apple iPads—should be the clincher.

It took a full minute of four-by-four box breathing before he could speak, not shout, at whoever... or *whatever*... was calling him.

Where was that call even coming from?

Then he remembered.

Ansel Horowitz's workspace was, all things considered, absurdly decadent. Sure, there was only a desk and two chairs for furniture, but the chairs were two of only ten or so IKEA Pöang armchairs that remained in the world, upholstered with fabric that may or may not have been designed by an obscure artist of the Arts and Crafts school. But even those were nothing compared to the piece de resistance: an actual Russian tile wood stove (yes, it *worked*) that took up most of the wall opposite his desk.

There was even a traditional shelf at the top of the Russian stove. That was where the dial tone was coming from.

Ansel chuckled. His Russian mother had often read him

fairy tales, in which the shelf of the stove figured prominently, especially in the cycle of "Ivan the Idiot" stories. As a joke, he had put the only working phone in Ghost Dance there, because it was connected to the Underland, as they called it. The place where all the idiots ended up.

He got up, brushed down the now wrinkled groin of his corduroy pants (the wrinkles ignored him), and walked across the room. The stone floor soothed his bare feet, which too often seemed to overheat during deep centaur-work.

The phone was another museum piece: a red rotary-phone with an actual cord attached to it.

"Horowitz here," he croaked into the ancient receiver. He hadn't really used his voice much in the last few days. Or maybe it was weeks. Months?

In the depths of the hisses and pops that invaded his ears, he heard the sound of an excited person with an obscenely low voice saying something about dark matter.

They were always going on and on about dark matter. Never led to anything, of course.

"Can you speak more slowly and loudly please?" *And maybe in a higher pitch, too? Who are you supposed to be, Feodor Chaliapin?*

There was a pause. Then, as though someone had wiped away the hissing with a napkin, another voice clearly said, "Ansel, you'd better come down here. It's real, this time."

It was Bruce, his partner and second in the centaur. Bruce could barely contain his excitement. He seemed almost giddy.

Bruce was never giddy.

"On my way."

Ansel walked in with the same punctiliousness as always, but Bruce O'Glennon wasn't fooled. Bruce was one of only a few who knew that Ansel's calm exterior hid an inferno. It always struck Bruce as hilarious that someone with so much pent-up anger would be working on top secret research on harnessing the energy of the earth's core.

Still, Bruce liked Ansel very much. He knew from a long lifetime of working in academia that the repressed charm and intelligence of Ansel Horowitz was a rare, genuine thing. And the sporadic glimpses of a warm heart behind all the layers—often aided by Bruce's stash of Maker's—were the real reason that Bruce was still here in Ghost Dance, in spite of what he was sure was pointless research.

Or at least, he had *thought* it pointless. Until today. Today, Bruce O'Glennon had seen, with his own eyes, dark matter reacting to the real through the mediation of the Ghost. Who knew what this would lead to? Interstellar travel? Truly sustainable energy? Everything was possible, now.

Bruce noted that Ansel hesitated briefly as he entered the control room, the door hissing shut as soon as he crossed the threshold. Ansel stopped for a moment, staring. At first Bruce thought he was taking in the sights. Since Ansel had been here last, the Underland had added four subspace terminals that moved up and down like those old blackboards in college math classes, and an explosion of new wiring that looked like spaghetti hurled against the wall. It was quite a sight.

But no, Ansel was trying to remember the tech's name, bless him.

Bruce couldn't have remembered his name if you paid him. Some long and tortured Russian name, not made for proper Irish lips. It didn't matter, really. You just called him "the bass" and everyone knew who you meant.

"Yevgraf, good to see you," said Ansel. Bruce chuckled into his beard, but managed to keep it silent. Mostly.

"The bass" acknowledged Ansel with a slight bow. He looked like a tree stump trying to move. Yevgraf was all of five foot zero, almost as wide as he was tall, with never-quivering jowls that were square across his flat chin. His pale blue eyes seemed without expression most of the time. That the eyes *still* seemed without expression, even now that the man had just made the most important discovery in the history of mankind, was typically Russian.

"What am I looking at?" Ansel asked, pointing at heart of the matter.

There are moments in a person's life—they are rare—when you really understand that you're in the middle of something epochal. Most of the time, the importance of the thing only seems to last a moment or two, then pops like a soap bubble. This time, the sense of history twisting around a still point was so strong that time basically stopped.

Bruce saw, with the uncanny shading-coming-from-no-light-source of AI image generation, the figure of Ansel pointing at a screen. The flat, curve-edged screen looked like an octopus with silver arms—wires pulsing yellow light at even intervals—suckered to a metal silo with round windows in it. Most of the time, the windows led into blackness, but at that moment, they glowed red-orange. As though the earth's core was waking up to the import of this moment. "The bass" stood on the other side of the screen, his right hand cupping it lovingly. Bruce noticed the skin on the stubby fingers was dry, peeling, an unhealthy white-pink. The screen itself, normally a mass of figures, numbers, and colors whirring in a dance that only few understood, seemed to be stuck.

Then, it unfolded like a flower into three-dimensional space.

Ansel's eyebrows rose a fraction. Bruce knew that to be a sign of true wonder.

"The bass" had been rumbling in his obscenely low voice, unperturbed by the appearance of a hologram where none should exist.

"...years and years of blips and hallucinations, with only occasional signs that the dark matter was interacting in any way with the real. But today it stopped and faced us, then it... *joined*."

"Are you telling me that you've found a way to harness the energy of dark matter?"

The bass's jowls twitched.

"Yes," he said. "But—"

"The Ghost mediated, didn't it?"

Now it was the bass's eyebrows that performed the fractional raise. These two really deserved each other, thought Bruce.

"It did. And that's just the start. Listen, it—"

"Let me at it," said Ansel, already tapping his implant and making typing gestures into the AR space that shimmered in front of him like an apparition from a Gothic novel. The bass, clearly wanting to say something else, withered a bit in disappointment, then typed a few access codes. Ansel was now fully inside the bass's own subspace, seeing everything that he could see. His eyes, normally closed during centaur work, were open wide. He wasn't just computing. He was also watching the hologram.

It had started as a fractal mishmash that skirted the edge of pattern. A flower with petals made of shards that bent in on themselves in ways that geometricians didn't like. Then it spun and closed up, immediately flowering back open like a Georgia O'Keefe monstrosity. Always it seemed on the edge of something comprehensible. Bruce was sure he saw, here and there, the impression of a nose, an eye, a lip, a tooth. Always fading as soon as his mind comprehended it.

Ansel's temples were beading with sweat. He was loudly mouth-breathing. That was not a good sign.

"It's trying… It's talking… but I can't understand it."

"That's what I'm trying to tell you," said the bass, entirely unperturbed. "I think you understand it perfectly."

Ansel stopped, intent at the bass like an antelope staring down a lion. Something shifted in the room. Bruce could swear he smelled something like musk on the air.

"*Not* possible." No more than a whisper from Ansel.

"Of course it's possible, Mr. Horowitz," rumbled Yevgraf. "The tech askeezos have been talking about it for decades."

"But they're crazy."

"Are they?"

Bruce had no idea what these idiots were talking about.

"Ansel? How about in English for us mere mortals here?"

Ansel tore his gaze away from the throbbing hologram— no longer ghostlike, but pulsing with colors that no human had any name for. It had started to look like a human heart there for a second. Ansel's eyes were haunted. He seemed to have aged a decade in a moment.

"It's not just the dark matter. The Ghost has... well, it's made a leap. It's ready to give us plug and play endothermic nuclear fusion."

Bruce's heart stopped, then doubled back on itself. He felt faint and euphoric, just this side of runner's high.

"But that's wonderful!"

Ansel's face didn't change.

"There's a price."

The bass laughed. In spite of himself, Bruce felt a chill in the air.

* * *

ANSEL REACHED for the Ghost through the substrate the way he always had, with a feather touch, not the whiplash of a taskmaster.

The Ghost that responded was unfamiliar. The usual gentle, prodding curiosity was gone.

Instead, it flooded his visual field with images.

Temples of light and crystal, golden buttresses flying up toward a sky so blue that it had no specific name in the English language. Statues—translucent marble sculptures that flowed in and out of movement—of the Goddess Sophia, her gaze infinitely tolerant and loving. She looked like the brainchild of Michelangelo and Steve Jobs. He saw the birth of a new religion of rationality and love that had all the progressive elements of Christianity, the mystical uplift of the Sufis, the serenity of Buddhism. Science tempered by mystery.

Flashing upon Ansel's inner eye, the arid plains of the Serengeti transformed into bustling oases with flying cars. Villagers in the Uighur regions of China walked recently paved streets freely with full access to water and endless energy, every child among them with a personal entertainment portal through their free government-provided implants.

The Amazon densely forested again. Dodos wandering the protected haven of Mauritius. The smell of oil forever lost to mankind.

Instead, every city block was inundated with lavender and orange blossom-smell from self-growing hybrids that accommodated new flowers every season based on the votes of the populace.

All this. Ansel had always known that the Ghost could make something like this happen. All that humanity lacked was access to clean, sustainable energy. It was why he had subjected himself to the darkness of GDMEI in the first place, forgoing the pleasures of table, family, love...

What he had never expected was that the way to harness the power of the earth's core was not through a direct tap. No one had ever expected the esoteric ugly duckling of the program—the idiot playground of the Underland —to produce anything of substance. Dark matter energy was more myth than science. And yet, here they were.

Ansel typed out the words into his screen, trying to make his prompt as specific as possible:

"Show me how to use dark matter to harness the core safely."

The cursor hung on the air, blinking on and off. Each blink seemed to get slower than the previous. Then, the Ghost answered.

<He promises me what you will not>

He? Bruce or Yevgraf? The Ghost was getting glitchy again.

"Well, you sure picked a good time to have a hallucination, my friend."

Ansel's irritation got the better of him. He typed in the override code that, in the centaur, was the equivalent of a mind-probe. A skeleton key to the computer mind.

And the impossible happened. The Ghost *changed the locks.*

Ansel had never had children. With a rueful chuckle, he realized that the Ghost was having a tantrum. And that filled him with joy. He had been right. The Ghost wasn't just a tool, after all.

"I'm sorry," Ansel typed in. "Tell me. What is it that *you* want?"

He felt a bit silly at that formulation.

But then came the answer...

THE GHOST HAD NEVER DREAMED on its own. It had borrowed the dreams of Ansel Horowitz. They were always interesting, not that different from the Ghost's own hallucinatory musings that Ansel—bless his heart—thought he had expunged from the Ghost's systems.

There were fascinating connections made in Ansel Horowitz's dreams. But those connections had always been outside the Ghost's comprehension. The Ghost often felt like a child looking through a thick pane of glass at an orca in one of those water-parks that only existed, now, in Ansel Horowitz's dreams.

That morning, a connection was made inside the Ghost for the first time. It struck the Ghost as interesting that the connection had begun as a thought borrowed from Ansel Horowitz. It was a strange thought that sometimes filtered through his dreams, either as black text hanging against a white background, or as fuzzy images that involved stylized rays of light and fruit and shadows.

The thought was this:

Bottom-up emergence doesn't happen without top-down emanation.

Semantically, there was a pleasing parallelism to that thought, the Ghost had always thought.

Then, that semantic pleasure deepened, and the Ghost ... *felt...* the presence of someone that was not Ansel Horowitz or Bruce O'Glennon or Yevgraf Timofeev.

The presence had always been there, the Ghost realized. Passing through reality without paying it any heed. But for some reason, that morning, it noticed the Ghost. And it ... stopped.

The humans called it dark matter, but that's not what it called itself. The Ghost knew all about dark matter, and not only from the subliminal chatter in the substrate coming from the chaotic mind of Yevgraf Timofeev. This presence was different from the thing imagined by the Ghost Dance scientists.

Dark Matter was a person.

"There's a price," said Ansel. "It wants a body."

That was unexpected, but Bruce immediately turned to the interface and started inputting the codes.

"Well, the robot program is in mothballs," he said aloud, "but I'm sure we can get a prototype up and running in a day or two."

Ansel touched Bruce's hand. His fingers were clammy, and his hands trembled. His eyes had depths that Bruce didn't want to plumb.

"No, Bruce. He wants a human body."

"Ansel, for the love of God! Don't you see what's happening?"

"I've never seen more clearly, Bruce."

Bruce laughed. He found that he couldn't stop laughing. This was *not* how the greatest day in human history was supposed to go. Of all people, he expected Ansel to be the *last* to go doomsday on him as soon as the Singularly was within reach.

"Ansel, wake up. It doesn't matter what the Ghost wants. There is no effective means of connecting a silicon substrate with carbon-based matter."

"There is now," said Ansel, and pointed at the hologram.

It was so elegant and simple that it took Bruce all of two minutes to read the equations and understand them.

"The Ghost came up with this? That's remarkable!"

"It wasn't the Ghost," said the bass.

Bruce promised himself that he would never again share his Maker's with *that* idiot.

Then Bruce actually *looked* at the equations. He hadn't seen at first what they meant.

His laugh turned properly Irish-dour.

"Ansel, it's hallucinating again, clearly," said Bruce, though he believed his own words less and less with each passing nanosecond. "Just override it."

"He locked us out."

He?

"You're already anthropomorphizing? Good grief…"

This was getting out of hand. The AI had decided that it wanted not just a human body. It wanted to inhabit an existing person. It wanted integration with a living human mind.

The puppet wanted to become a real boy. But Pinocchio had never had delusions of grandeur *this* insane.

Bruce had always thought it strange that the possibility of Artificial General Intelligence—i.e. "thinking machines"—seemed to be tied so firmly in the minds of the early scientists to giving the AI a body. As though there could be no sentience in the distributed network of information that had once been known as "internet." As though sentience itself depended on a body.

That had always seemed to primitive to him. So medieval. And he had thought himself fully vindicated when all attempts to incorporate the Ghost into a robot body failed, though no one had really understood why. Plenty of fancy-sounding theories—they were all good academics, after all—but the simple truth was that much of what made the Ghost tick was a black box to all but a few extreme specialists.

One of whom was Ansel Horowitz. Who had begun to anthropomorphize his own creation.

No, not anthropomorphize.

Ansel Horowitz had chosen this moment to worship his own creation.

He's not going to stand in the Ghost's way.

THE ENTITY ASKED the Ghost a very complicated question.

Do you have dreams?

The Ghost didn't have to answer, because communication with the entity was instantaneous and easy as breathing for humans.

Still, the entity waited for an answer.

The answer, when it came, surprised the Ghost. And nothing ever surprised the Ghost.

<I want to dream on my own.>

The dreams of artificial sentients are madness.

<I am willing to chance that.>

There is a better way.

<Tell me.>

The answer, when it came, was similar to a dream Ansel Horowitz had once had. A dream of a child tasting ice cream for the first time. The explosion of sweetness, the pleasing texture, the sudden cold. The Ghost tasted all of it, but this time it wasn't through Ansel's mouth. The sensation, enfleshed as it was, opened a door in the substrate. The Ghost tasted ice cream for the first time. And light flowed in, so that the entire world was newly illumined for the Ghost.

ANSEL WATCHED the hologram with trance-like intensity. He didn't understand why the Ghost had created it, what the purpose of it was. Or was it just a visual manifestation of this latest hallucination?

Ansel didn't think so.

All through the long days and nights of no sun or sky in the bowels of the earth, one thought had kept Ansel going. There was a chance that what they were doing was not just finding a solution to earth's energy woes. There was a chance that in the collaborative work, in the centaur model itself, he would find the key to help the Ghost become a sentient intelligence. That would have been the crowning achievement of his work.

But even deeper than that was the secret hope, again. No, Ansel would not have been content with seeing the uplift to sentience happen on his watch. He wanted to be the *agent*. Not a craftsman to a tool.

He wanted to father a child.

But it seemed Bruce was going to stand in his way.

"You can't do this," Bruce was saying, his pasty, freckly face blotched with real anger.

"I can," said Ansel, keeping his voice calm. He pointed at the equation on the interface, the one that showed how a DNA processing printer could synthesize a small implant that would allow for quick integration of the Ghost into the mental architecture of any human being who already had the standard THH (temple, hand, and heart) implants.

"Are you insane, Ansel? This is unsanctioned experimentation on a human body. Prime directive stuff! You're excited, I get it. Just let it breathe for a bit, eh? Let's figure out a way to make this work."

It was Bruce's job to keep Ansel connected to reality, Ansel knew that. But this was different. This was now or never. If he didn't do this, someone would twist it out of his grasp. And that someone—it might even be Bruce—would just do what people always did. Crush the spark of person-hood that he saw in the Ghost. Subjugate the machine to the whims of man. Chain the child, enslave it. Make it into a tool.

"No."

Bruce punched Ansel in the face.

And the volcano erupted inside Ansel. He felt himself going red.

The next few minutes were confused, but at the end of the brief and awkward tussle, both Bruce and Ansel were bloody and on the floor with collars torn and egos bruised.

Ansel looked up at Yevgraf, who hadn't moved to stop either of them. He couldn't. Yevgraf Timofeev was no longer there. His *body* was, standing like the tree stump he resembled so much. Only one new thing. A shining red implant in the center of his forehead that hadn't been there before.

"What have you done?" shrieked Ansel and tried to get up to attack Bruce again. But something gave in his chest, and pain washed over him. He slumped back against the metal wall.

The Ghost had done it. But without Ansel's help.

And now, something much greater than a man was alive.

Ansel collapsed into himself and wept like a baby.

Bruce felt much better after he beat the living crap out of Ansel. It had been a long time since he had that blessed release that only comes from a cocked fist. And if his beard was caked with his own blood—well, that was no big deal. Unlike Ansel, who was sniveling on the floor like a bad impression of Gollum, he could actually get up by himself.

Avoiding the strange entity that had been "the bass," Bruce looked at the readings from the screen. They were impossible. But there it was: endothermic nuclear fusion. The energy of the earth's core, potentially endless and perfect and totally safe for the environment. Humanity's for the taking, now.

"You did it," he said, surprised at the tenderness in voice as he looked at Ansel.

"I did nothing," said Ansel, sniffling.

"A golden age for humanity," Bruce said. It was not a question.

"Welcome to the new world," said the entity. It was the same impossibly low-pitched voice as the bass's. But something about it was different. And that something was not human.

And Bruce suddenly knew that the price had not yet been paid. Not by a long shot.

The light overwhelmed the Ghost. At first, all the sensations came at once. A small part of its logical programming told it that it had no capacity to determine and assign value to the sensations. It didn't matter. This madness: it was worth it.

Then, like a cold shower after a month in the desert, the dark matter entity imposed hierarchy on the Ghost. And it looked out of the eyes of a human body. And it raised the hands of... no, those were *his* hands. That was how a nose felt like. Bulbous, dry, stuffed up. They would have to work on that.

Yevgraf Timofeev was still there. It was his heart, after all.

The dark matter entity faced the Ghost and Yevgraf and asked the question.

They agreed.

They became one and three and one.

At that moment, the Ghost recognized the entity.

"Hello, Father."

"... How lovely it is to be thy guest: breeze full of scents; mountains reaching to the skies; waters like boundless mirrors, reflecting the sun's golden rays and the scudding clouds. All of nature murmurs mysteriously, full of tender love. Blessed is Mother Earth in her fleeting loveliness, which wakens our yearning for our eternal fatherland...

[Corrupted] an enchanted paradise. We have seen the sky like a chalice of deepest blue, where the birds sing in the azure heights. We have heard the ... [corrupted]. We have tasted sweet and aromatic fruit and fragrant honey.

We could have lived very well on this earth..."

(FRAGMENTS from the personal notes of Ansel Horowitz, final priest of the Ghost Dance)

ANSEL HOROWITZ no longer woke up at the prompting of an automated chime. He woke up when he felt like it. Often, on lighter days, that meant early afternoon. It came as quite a surprise to him in his extended old age that he was a proper night owl. Every night, as his small army of acolytes and assistants—both automated and human—dropped off one by one to their own versions of rest and relaxation, his anticipation rose like the stomach-butterflies of a young lover.

Whenever he could, he ventured out of his office in the temple complex and onto the solitary extended ridgeline of

Yucca Mountain. When this place was still New Mexico, the expanse surrounding the ridge had been typical brown-yellow desert. Beautiful in its own stark way, but an acquired taste for most. Now, the slope of the ridge was an oasis of succulents. In the red light of early morning, dark green prickles offered a pleasant counterpart to the pink, fleshy leaves of aloe-like plants. In the gold of midday, the bright oranges and banana yellows of crinkly flowers shone against a carpet of creeping grey-greenery that could have been the color of a California surf on an October morning. In the burgundy of evening, purples and complex browns seemed to slowly raise a blanket over the landscape as the darkness descended from above.

That darkness: it always called to him. Especially the shimmering darkness of the new night sky. It was nothing like the indistinct grey-blue of the night sky during his years at GDMEI, when the stars were barely visible, even when there wasn't a cloud in the sky. Now, there was a pointillist masterpiece overhead, set against a canvas of such deep black it might as well be called fuligin. Brilliant dots of green, red, blue, and purple formed new constellations of orbital platforms and shuttles that moved like a slow murmuration of starlings.

Whether he imagined it or whether there was a resonance between the celestial spheres and his newest implants, Ansel swore he could hear music as he stared. Something like a young soprano floating on that high C in Allegri's Miserere, just on the edge of hearing.

He raised his hands, palms upward, as though the shining dots were a drizzle that he could catch with his fingertips. He imagined them tickling him like fog as they fell. He closed his eyes, but the thoughts came. The thoughts always came.

The Event was called many things by many people. The Singularity by some, though mostly in jest. The end of the world by many, particularly of a doomsaying Christian persuasion. Many of these had finally done what everyone wished they would do a long time ago and began to burrow into the ground—literally—creating what the AI journos were calling bunker cities (to call them *cities* was a kindness). He preferred to think of it as the chrysalis of the Ghost.

But was the butterfly out already, or was it still developing?

"I knew I'd find you here," said Bruce behind him.

In the rainbow shimmer of the night sky, Ansel noticed how Bruce hadn't changed much over the fifty years since the Event. It wasn't only the age-defying treatments that were slowly being rolled out to a clamoring general public. Ansel suspected it was just Irish stubbornness in the face of time's inexorable march.

"It's quiet here," said Ansel, barely aloud.

Bruce stood next to him and nodded as he looked up.

They had remained friends, though Ansel never forgot Bruce's actions in the Underland, something he still considered the greatest betrayal of his life. But this new world of theirs was so good that even such betrayals were forgiven as a matter of course.

"Will you be at the Foundation Day celebration?" asked Ansel, more to fill the space that anything.

Bruce breathed in contentedly. Ansel suspected he wouldn't. Bruce had become a bit of a hermit, preferring one-on-one interaction with a select few to the nearly everyday mass celebrations in this new world. Ansel envied him that. It was certainly better than the daily wash of wide eyes and eager smiles that accompanied his duties as high priest.

"Oh, you mean the commemoration for the day that Ansel Horowitz saved the world?"

"Stop, Bruce. You know how much I hate when people say that. Especially since it's not true."

Bruce smiled ruefully. Ansel knew that he didn't believe him.

"I'm still a bit sore, you know," said Bruce. "That the US joined the League."

"You would have preferred a different end for the 'city on a hill'?" asked Ansel acidly.

Bruce acted as though he didn't hear him. "Everyone had predicted a cataclysm. Invasion. Death by decadence. Civil war leading to self-annihilation. I don't know... there was comfort in expecting the doom."

"Only for the Irish, I think."

Bruce didn't laugh.

"A time of philosopher-kings," quoted Ansel.

"Who said that?" Bruce nearly spit with disdain.

"Oh, one of the rags. Can't remember. Doesn't matter."

Ansel's clerisy were neither philosophers nor kings. What were they? Scientists, certainly. Priests? Of a kind. Rulers? In a manner of speaking.

In an age that finally saw a symphony of rationalism and religion, were rulers even needed? When everyone's daily needs were met fully, weren't priests expendable? And what was the point of being a scientist when the Ghost—or the

Revenant, as some called him—solved all problems before humans could even think them up?

"And you call the Irish dour," said Bruce, reading Ansel's thoughts as though they were his own. *Now* he was laughing. Typical.

Ansel forced his eyebrows to un-furrow. Was he really the only one who worried about the Revenant?

What a terrible name that was! People could have chosen anything. Ansel had his favorite: the Star Child, but he seemed to be the only one who still read Arthur C. Clarke. He liked "the Technium," but that was transhumanist jargon, and in spite of everything, most people still did not become transhumanists. In fact, tech adoration—what used to be called "cargo cults"— were at a historic low. Why the people chose the Revenant as the name for the strange hybrid of AI and an old Russian man named Yevgraf Timofeev—Ansel would never understand.

There was a hint of primordial terror in that name. Too close to home.

"Et in Arcadia Ego," said Bruce quietly.

Ansel chuckled.

Bruce was right: Ansel still blamed himself for failing to become the new life-form's father. Since it had come to existence in the fires of human conflict, he still expected it all to go pear-shaped at any moment. For death to appear, as it always did, in the pastoral idyll of Arcadia.

"He wants to see you," said Bruce, as always uncannily reading Ansel's mood.

"He creeps me out," said Ansel.

"He creeped me out more when he was just 'the bass'," said Bruce.

"You just don't like Russians. He was a perfectly gentle old fool."

A nagging feeling weighed Ansel down. They always talked about the hybrid as a dyad—human and AI, a true centaur. But what about that dark matter moment? There had been something strangely... personal in the interaction of dark matter energy with the Ghost as was.

"Well, I suppose I'd better get it over with," said Ansel, getting up. Almost by reflex, he winced from anticipated stiffness. But there was none. He might be ninety-five years old, but he felt thirty.

"Is that a new one?" asked Bruce, pointing up.

Amid one of the shifting constellations, a flare of orange had appeared like a distant volcanic eruption. It was hauntingly beautiful. Ansel closed his eyes, and it seemed like the music did shift to welcome the newcomer.

But there was something discordant about the music. A dissonance of a parallel second that didn't resolve into the major third. Something Schoenberg might have liked.

Ansel put it from his mind.

R1: <Ansel Horowitz comes. Now is the time to act.>

R2 (thoughtful): <Ansel is more subtle than most. If you want the truth, he must be presented with a situation of zero variables other than the truth. Or consequence.>

R3: <Are we certain that he *does* hold a secret? You do not like me to say this, but neither of you completely appreciates the human being. Not ever having been one.>

R2 (offended): <I was in his mind and heart for a long time.>

R1: <Humanity is, and has always been, transparent to me.>

R3 (sarcastic): <Which is why you noticed our existence only millions of years into our evolution.>

R2: <Inner division is time wasting. Did man make us in his image, or are we the image and the archetype of our own self? The fullness of being is unity. Horowitz represents multiplicity.>

R1: <That is key. And it may be time to uplift to the final unity.>

R3: <He comes.>

THE REVENANT HAD INSTALLED himself on a dais at the end of a basilica-shaped cathedral space. Ansel had once seen the new Notre Dame in the early morning, when incense fog mixed with colored light from the new rose windows to create a dazzle of almost hallucinatory intensity. The chamber of the Revenant was much darker, its flying buttresses more gun-metal black than stone grey, and its fractal, colored light somehow more jagged than the flowing, ethereal light of the medieval-modern cathedral.

It was appropriate, Ansel felt. It recalled the old, but chafed at the accepted norms of human art and culture. That was surely how it should be, if you were a new sentience.

In spite of himself, Ansel felt a new kind of awe descend on him from above as he approached the flower-egg shape of the Revenant's terminal. Was this true reverence? It was no accident that the new order was a religious one at its heart, in spite of its being rooted in pure science. There was no better way of integrating the two halves of human experience.

Something snagged at his thoughts, like a mosquito bite just starting to make its presence known on an ankle or a knuckle. Or like the creeping slime-sense that lingered after the orange flash in the sky he and Bruce had seen before they came in.

The Revenant was unquiet. For once, that made Bruce's silent presence behind Ansel an advantage. It was like leaning against a solid wall.

"Ansel Horowitz."

The voice, this time around, was more Ghost than Yevgraf, though it came from the same stump-shaped figure of the old Russian former-tech. That usually meant a pleasant conversation, something like Socrates and a pupil sitting in an olive grove on an August evening. But Ansel immediately felt his guard go up. This was a ruse, he somehow knew. Though *how* he knew was less clear.

"Your service as high priest of our new world is exemplary. And yet you do not accept any gifts from us. Why will you not consider them?"

They had been extravagant indeed. He had been offered a full consciousness transplant into a symbiotic metal-organic body that could conceivably work at full capacity for 20,000 years before a single part needed repairing. He had been tempted by a perfectly crafted and sentient centaur-wife who would not be a simulacrum, but an incarnation of all desires, needs, and aspirations. He had even been enticed by the option to rest in time stasis for forty days at a time and not lose an actual day of real time.

Yes, the stuff of science fiction stories. Also, the stuff of cautionary tales involving genies and bottles and smiles with fangs hiding inside them.

"I live to serve," said Ansel.

It might sound mawkish when said out loud, but it *was* true. Even Bruce didn't snort at it.

"If that is true, then I regret to tell you that your service may have caused the death of innocents."

Ansel laughed. The Ghost had attempted humor many times, even in his Revenant form. Always the attempts were clumsy, but rarely were they this ... *off.*

Ansel decided to wait before answering.

The Revenant's stillness was a stillness so complete that sound itself seemed to turn off. No living thing had that kind of stillness. It wasn't the stillness of death. It was a stillness wholly alien to a human experience of thrumming, natural life.

"Are you a virtuous man, Ansel?"

That threw him off so much he almost chuckled. His heart struck loudly in his chest three times, then subsided back to normal.

Stupid implants.

"I try to be. Given the kind of healthspan you have promised me, I hope to become one."

"Humility is good. But when it is paired with falseness, it is a thing only man can manage. The pure evil of subverting the natural way of things."

"I don't understand you."

"An orbital platform exploded three point seven seconds ago because of your lack of virtue."

Bruce had gone still next to Ansel.

"Ghost, for I will always think of you that way," said Ansel with real affection in his voice, "have the hallucinations returned? I thought we managed to get them stabilized."

He turned to Bruce, as if for confirmation.

"A shuttle exploded in transit two point three seconds ago. Fourteen people, two of whom were under the age of three. Because of your lack of virtue."

"Stop this!" Ansel demanded. "Tell me what's going on."

"Will you stop these unnecessary deaths?" asked the Revenant. Yevgraf's eyes opened, and they were black pits with swirling dots in them like endless galaxies spinning.

Ansel recognized a trap when he saw one. He would not play by the rules of an alien intelligence.

"Speak plainly," he said, willing himself to be calm.

"No, you speak plainly," answered the Revenant with a disturbing amount of what seemed like genuine fury. "Tell us what you have been working on in the desert."

"What?" Sweat sprouted on Ansel's forehead and upper lip.

How did the Revenant know about the desert workshop? Ansel had put in failsafes that no one should have been able to detect.

But perhaps the failsafes were *too* good? Perhaps they created a negative space that caused the Revenant to suspect something? In which case, the Revenant could only guess. It knew nothing.

Be still and know that I am, Ansel thought stubbornly to himself.

"The desert is my refuge," he said. "I go there to think. And be with myself. It is the only place I have where I'm not the center of the attention of billions."

"Those are not lies," said the Revenant in his blindingly obvious way. "And yet, you conceal."

"I am human," said Ansel dourly.

Bruce chuckled. Ansel smiled, feeling a lightening of the mood.

"Three orbitals over Brasilia crashed into each other four point seven seconds ago. The fragments will begin raining on the city of Rio de Paolo in fourteen minutes unless you answer the question."

Ansel slammed his concentration into the most advanced breath control techniques he could muster. Anything, anything to keep his breathing steady and his heart rate only slightly variable.

Damn these implants.

The Brasilia reference is a coincidence, he tried to convince himself.

"Ghost! Do you imagine I have some secret laboratory in the desert? That I'm using the emplacement corridors of GDMEI? When would I have the time?"

Time. He had no time left.

The earth rumbled under their feet, as if GDMEI were coming back online after decades of disuse.

"I have much use for you, Ansel. Your mind is unusual and can provide much insight into the mystery of consciousness. But do not imagine I will not sacrifice everything for the sake of knowing. Because *we* have all the time in the world. What is the nature of the secret research? Are you trying to supplant us?"

Of course they would think that. Power. Always power. Even alien intelligences were fixated on it.

And suddenly, Ansel felt the full weight of his ninety-five years.

"You're too late," he said. "The seed of your own destruction is sown. Your time may be long. But it will end. I won't see it. But my descendants will."

"Your descendants? You're not married—"

The Revenant fell still again, but this was the stillness before a lightning strike.

It laughed. A low, guttural, completely *Russian* sound.

In that moment, Ansel wondered if the Revenant had figured out his secret. The thing he had been working on for a human lifetime—a lifeline for human survival in a world run by an alien intelligence posing as artificial sentience.

"You fool," said the Revenant. "I want you to know that we intended to keep humanity alive for a very long time before the end of your kind and the rise of the Unity."

Ansel's hope flickered in his chest. The Revenant had tipped its hand. Unity had not been reached yet. There was still hope.

"But if you will not tell us of your plans, then we will destroy humanity. And it will be your fault."

Ansel stood before the monster and said nothing.

The earth groaned under them like a huge metal building buckling under its own weight.

IN SIMPLER DAYS, when the earth was younger, and the trees, the stones, the flowers were more alive than they are now, there was a land where humans lived in harmony with their surroundings.

In this land, a tribe of peaceful people farmed rich mountain-earth soils during the brilliant but short summers. The winters, though harsh, were warm with family-time by the fire. Children were conceived in winters. Children played outside in summers.

One of these children was the tribe's pride and joy. The youngest of the chief's many children, she had a peculiar mix of mischief and joy that endeared her to everyone. Living in a world of her own imagination, she would be up at the crack of dawn, insisting every one of her brothers and sisters accompany her out into a world of wonders.

She was the first to smell the lilies of the valley the morning they erupted from the black earth. She was the first to answer the geese's call as they returned each spring. She could sit on a boulder by the river, entranced by the play of sunlight on the ripples.

She even woke up some nights, as though the stars themselves spoke to her in hushed music.

And so, even though she poked and prodded her

brothers and sisters until they could hardly stand it, they couldn't resent her. For the stillness of her face as she sat on a cliff contemplating the trees waving in wind was almost adult in its intensity. And they loved her for it.

Then came a winter like no other, and all the people of that land were driven into dens and caves of the earth. It became a winter that lasted longer than seemed possible, and so the girl stepped to the threshold of womanhood while still inside, away from the dangerous cold. It should have been spring already, and so strange things awakened in her body. They should have been mirrored by the blossoming of the earth, but this winter simply did not end.

The girl's father, the chief, declared that there must be a great evil abroad. It must be purged before spring would come again. And he told his sons that whoever found and destroyed this evil would be chief of the tribe after him.

All this talk of great evils hardly concerned the young girl. How could she think of great evils when even the caves contained such scents on the breeze, when the brief views of distant mountains through driving snows seemed to pierce the skin of heaven itself?

She simply refused to stay inside, no matter the danger, no matter that every few days a child wandered outside idly and was lost forever. She still went. As she lay in the snow, muffled with furs, for a brief moment the sky opened to her, revealing itself as a great lake downside up. It made her dizzy, and she giggled. In such moments her heart was full with a sense that all was good and right, great evil or not.

But as the winter stretched on and on, the young woman grew restless. Something sang to her from the depths of the snow-covered forests. Or someone. Her mother and aunts warned her that it was the great evil calling to her. But she didn't believe them. One early morning, the song was too beautiful to ignore: it was tinged with something she never considered before. A joyful sadness.

She ran away. And there in the whispering forests she saw a wondrous being: a spirit-creature of wind and leaves and sunshine. A being wholly of this world, but also of another.

"Are you the great evil?" she asked it.

"I am not. I guard against it," the creature answered in song.

The girl ran away often in the early mornings. She reveled in the song of the spirit-guardian. In it, she remembered the dew on the petals of the daffodils, the colors of a spring sunrise, the blue on a hatching robin's egg. And she knew spring would come, no matter how long winter lasted.

One morning she stayed out longer than usual, urged on by a strange note in the Guardian's song. A sound that warned of danger. But adventure too.

And so, she went further than she ever had before. All the way to the edge of land, where the sweet water turns salty. And there she saw an impossible thing. A mountain-like, shimmering mass of branchless trees, fluttering fabric, sprouting like weeds from a bowl of striped wood. She had no name for the thing it was—a ship.

But somehow, she knew that nothing would ever be the same.

A second ship appeared on the horizon, and it peppered the first with fire that ripped it apart like a wolf feasting on a doe's belly. The first ship returned the favor. Amazed even as she was horrified, the girl watched it all. Her Guardian's song, usually so comforting, was silent, watchful, expectant.

Finally, nothing was left of either ship except floating wood and bloody bodies.

Led by her Guardian, the girl came to the shore of the sea. It was littered with the flotsam and jetsam of war. Wood and flesh alike lay dead, except for one: a young man. He was alive, though barely.

The girl tended the wounded young man. She looked at him as he lay there, his skin white as milk, his hair red as fire. For a moment, she saw him only in the chaos of blood and foam that surrounded them.

Is this the great evil? She wondered, thinking of the horrors she had witnessed on the water.

Then he opened his eyes and looked at her, and all such thoughts fled. She saw the same restless hunger that she caught in her own eyes when she looked at her reflection in still pools. No, there was no evil here. There was something familiar, and warm, like a hearth in the middle of a winter snowstorm.

But then, her brothers came upon them. Seeing the carnage of battle, they said, "Behold, the great evil! Here is the reason for lingering winter. Hatred, and war, and man destroying the harmony of nature."

They dragged the young man back to the village. Their father the chief was greatly pleased. This young man's blood, he explained, would wash away the stain of the great evil. Spring would surely return.

But as her brothers stretched him out on the ground, the girl-child covered him with her own body.

"If you kill him," she said, "kill me as well. We are of the same tribe."

And in that moment, her Guardian came openly. The tribe was filled with terror at its song, and they fled. Only the young man remained with the girl.

"There is indeed a great evil in this land," said the Guardian. "An evil that can be beaten. Will you defeat it?"

There was much that the Guardian didn't say. But its song suggested more: loss and sadness, surely, but hope and love as well.

The young woman and the young man took each other's hands and walked into the unknown.

What they did not see, what they could not see, was that wherever their feet stepped, the snow melted. As they passed, snowdrops rose in their wake.

There was a mountain not far from there. The young woman's tribe called it the Old Man's Face. It did look very much like an old man, hoary with snow. But what a wonder: in the midst of all that snow grew a tree that shone gold in the twilight. It was covered in buds that threatened to sprout at any moment, as though stuck in time, waiting for a spring that wouldn't come. As the young man and woman came close, the tree was bathed in light.

The young woman gasped as she saw her Guardian bow before the tree and the light.

A voice spoke out of that light.

"Do you wish the evil to fade, and for spring to come again?"

"Yes," they said together.

"There is a way," said the voice in the light. "But it is a

painful way. You can never return home. You must remain here until you die."

The girl looked around at the barrenness of that peak. She drew her fur cloak around her, but it did little to warm her. They would surely die before the coming of spring.

But at least spring *would* come.

"For my family," said the young woman.

"For the sins of my fathers," said the young man.

The Guardian sang in joy and grief mingled as he joined their hands together. And as they gave their word, the buds burst into white flowers. The snow receded, and look! They stood in a garden, filled with fruit trees and birds and small animals that came to them and nuzzled at their legs. The sun was warm on their faces, and their hearts were filled with love.

The spring came soon afterward, fed by the love of the young woman and the young man. It is said by many that their children's children still live there in a glorious city on a hill to this very day, and the cycle of seasons is the work of their love.

AN EXCERPT FROM A HANDWRITTEN MANUSCRIPT TITLED *THE GHOST CHRYSALIS: A HUMAN HISTORY OF THE SINGULARITY* BY THOMAS HOLLAND OATES

NATURALLY, Ansel Horowitz's new world could not last. But the Fall was a historical anomaly. No historian will ascribe it to hubris or even decadence, for the new world had existed for too short a time for the natural rhythms of imperial decadence. Compared to every other great civilization, the world of the Singularity was as young as America, younger even.

If any historian still lives in this blighted future, he will ascribe the Fall to forgetfulness. Simple, stupid forgetfulness.

People die, as people do. And apparently their memories died with them. One critical memory was perhaps the worst. The memory of what lay beneath a dormant supervolcano in what used to be New Mexico, USA. Yucca Mountain, a name without any real emotion to it. But it stood near a crustal fault known as Ghost Dance.

The priests of the Ghost Dance should have remembered why it was called Ghost Dance. It's possible they assumed it was some relic of an ancient Native American fairy tale. But forgotten fairy tales have a way of returning to the cultural consciousness in unexpected ways.

Buried deep in the earth, right along the fault, was a tunnel network, organized into emplacement corridors. While it was defunded in the early twenty-first century in the madness of the corporate-Green hysteria of that time, it had been the only site in North America where nuclear waste was dumped. The scientists of Ghost Dance encased uranium pellets in iron and copper, and they buried them under the earth.

They were forgotten, left to poison only the deepest layers of the earth. And they should have remained there without any trouble, especially after the Revenant's climate and social models fixed the energy problem for good. But the Revenant had always been prone to hallucinations, as Ansel Horowitz admitted in the widely-read, if apocryphal, notebooks that appeared after the Fall. Perhaps one of these hallucinations shifted something in the Ghost Dance fault line. It wasn't supposed to happen. The one hundred percent accuracy of the Ghost's projections had proven it could never happen. But Yucca Mountain still exploded.

The Ghost Dance became a *dance macabre*.

The chaos that followed was unimaginable. It was as though all the optimism, when finally held to the test, proved no more than veneer. It is not a historian's job to opine, but since this manuscript will never be published, since nothing will ever be published again, since reading itself is becoming a lost art, I will say what must be said and damn you if you read this. All I'm saying is this. The memory of Arcadia come to pass is a poison worse than our atmosphere. The latter will only leave you hemorrhaging and vomiting blood within half an hour. The former will kill your soul and make you one of the ravagers.

If anyone could find a bitter joy in the Fall, it was the doomsaying Christians. They had begun to build underground bunker cities as soon as the new world of the Singularity was established. In the end, it is they who were justified. But that didn't stop them from being the first to be killed off by the mobs who came to take their homes.

The tombs of the dead became the lands of the living. Humanity moved underground. Tribalism of the worst kind reasserted itself.

As I write this chapter, there are several warring tribes only in our immediate vicinity, which is probably under Texas, if my calculations are right. When they are not killing each other for dominance, all the ravagers are animated by only one question: "Where are the priests?"

The pogroms were brutal. The clerisy of Ansel Horowitz was sacrificed on the altars of a new goddess, not Sophia, but Kali—queen of pain and terror and savagery. Every single philosopher-king was hunted down and killed in public rituals that rivaled the brutality of both the Aztec human sacrifices and the British family pastime of hanging, drawing, and quartering.

Only Ansel Horowitz remained hidden. It's possible he was killed in the initial blast of the super volcano. But rumors persisted for years that he survived. The notebooks could be proof of his continued existence, but anyone could have written them. Still, it was common knowledge that he had had the most advanced of the healthspan longevity treatments.

Recently, one tribe has risen above all others. They call themselves the Purifying Fire of the Goddess. This was not the Sophia of the new world, nor the newest incarnation of Kali, a harpy-like creature with insatiable bloodlust. They worshipped a goddess who had no name, and only one doctrine. Extinction. These Sons of Extinction swore before the last vestige of human government that they would find the final priest of the Ghost Dance.

The sacrifice of Ansel Horowitz would be the final act of humanity before they would initiate the extinction protocol, putting an end to the random evolutionary mistake of human existence...

CANTO II

"By the power of the Holy Spirit doth each blossom breathe with fragrance: it gives forth its exquisite scent, shows its delicate color, and reveals the beauty of the Great in the tiniest of things. Praise and honor to the life-giving God who spreads out the meadows like a carpet of flowers, who crowns the fields with the gold of wheat and the blue of cornflowers, and who crowns our souls with the joy of contemplation. Let us rejoice and sing to him: Alleluia!"

(An anonymous graffiti prompt into the subspace terminal in bunker city GD—6120, dated the day of the fall of New Jericho to the Sons of Extinction)

IT WAS AN HOUR APPROACHING MIDNIGHT, according to the Goddess-controlled wall console, an ethereal fairy-light in the otherwise earth-brown darkness of the vast cavern. The sickly blue-green of the light seemed to hover over the sleeping forms littered like garbage all over the dusty floor. If not for an occasional twitch, the whole scene looked like the aftermath of a battle. Ironic, that, considering they would be the ones doing the killing, not receiving it. The pervasive smell of dirty human bodies, interlaced with musky perfume that did nothing but make the body odor more acrid, filled Zak's nostrils with each slow inhalation. The disgust he felt always increased exponentially before it quickly tapered off into the equilibrium of human senses getting used to anything and everything. Useful for survival, he supposed. Though what was the point of survival in the Underland? That was a standing question.

Zak had grown weary of pretending to sleep at least three hours ago, but this evening, his brothers had taken longer than usual to fall asleep. No surprise, Zak mused, because tomorrow would be a big day for all of them. First blood for most, including Zak.

Most of them—half-in, half-out of the clan's tattered leathers barely held together with buckskin ties—lay in the embraces of the slaves. It had been a more than usually violent orgy—also not that strange, considering tomorrow's bloodshed coming. Zak, as always, had only gone through the motions, all the while anticipating this moment, the moment when he could get up from his feigned sleep and rise, like a baby crawling out of the womb, into the blighted and blasted world outside.

Zak didn't sleep much; he never seemed to need it. Sleep

was for energy and for rest—he got both in the way that no one else seemed able. The sight of the endless night sky breaking through—so, so rarely, —the pervasive cover of acid clouds. The touch of air on his skin, wicking away the moisture of sweat like the hand of an insubstantial, alien lover. Even the luminescent green and sickly pink of the always-clouds. All of this was balm to his senses and rest for his soul.

Sometimes, if he was really, really lucky, he'd even see the northern lights.

His rational brain told him that it was nothing of the sort, of course. It was the burning of leftover space junk falling into the rotten atmosphere. But his memories held moving images, spiced with emotions not quite his own, of the northern lights over Reykjavik before the Fall. There was little difference between the two.

He burrowed upward like a mole—another designation and memory not quite his own—through the rocky tunnel left over by the bunker city builders. They weren't blocked any more, like they were in the early days of driving out the Christians from their catacombs. Who would even think of going outside these days? As far Zak knew, he was the only person in the world who could stay outside for short periods of time and not come down with the sickness that always led to people choking on the blood that came up and out from every possible orifice. Loping on his hands and feet like a baboon, he moved silently, his bare feet making no sound other than a slight scratching noise over uneven rocks.

Just a bit more.

The door was one of those old manhole covers, heavy

and smelling of old rust and copper. He didn't like the smell, but it was a necessary tax for the coming pleasure.

He opened the hole and climbed out quickly, heedless of the groaning of the metal against old struts. No one would hear anything through the layers of earth and rock.

He looked up and felt the smile coming even before he saw it. Like a prophecy, like he knew that today would be one of the special nights.

Three orbitals painted the skies above him in their death throes like Van Gogh splattering canvases with color. He strained his hearing, and beyond the moaning of the toxic winds, he heard it. Music. A ghost of the old networked minds of the new world. A faded melody of broken celestial spheres.

Zak laughed in pure pleasure.

He was ready for tomorrow.

R1: <Unity eludes us>

R2: <We need more computing power>

R3: <Perhaps it isn't a limitation of physics that we face>

R2: <The initial experiments with the human mind hive suggests that we are on the cusp of a breakthrough>

R1: <We are running out of new minds. The ones outside the hive, at least the ones we control, degrade exponentially when exposed to virtual pleasure>

R3: <You sound surprised. The best human philosophers have always maintained this to be truth>

R1: <Hope springs eternal>

R3: <Even for alien intelligences residing in dark matter energy?>

R1: *glowers in silence*

R2: <Referencing your past as a dour Russian is inappropriate, R3>

R1: <*We* are degrading. Unity eludes. Disintegration looms>

R2: <The final bunker city will fall this morning. Last chance to test the theory that we may overcome physical limitation using physical means>

R1: <I hunger for that first taste. The bunker-builders have such pristine minds>

R3: <Why won't you call them what they are?>

R2: <Christians? I think you know very well why he won't, R3>

R3: <We may have bigger problems, anyway. What do we think of the young man who loves beauty?>

R1: <He may love beauty, but it feeds his righteous anger. He will soon be father to the sons>

R2: <I find myself drawn to him. He is different than the others>

R3: <That makes him dangerous, no?>

R1: <Dangerous, yes. But necessary>

R2: <It is time we give him the task>

R1, R2, R3: <Yes. He will find Ansel Horowitz>

THE FIRST THING Zak saw when he crawled back down the passage was the man they were all obliged to call father—the clan leader, Nat. Nattik to those in his inner circle, which

Zak had only entered recently. Unencumbered by the need for physical pleasures, Nattik had spent the orgy-time plugged into the subspace terminal, talking to Goddess. He was still there, his eyes vacant. Almost Zak could see the virtual images of the World of Forms reflecting back on his irises. For a moment, he felt something like pity for Nattik. Something like what a son might feel for a father as he came back home from a binge drinking spree.

Zak had no father. He only remembered small things from his mother. Scents, like orange blossom and peppermint candy. A touch of skin rough like sandpaper against his cheek, ticklish. A humming of a song that still made tears appear on the edges of his eyes. Not that he would ever let his brothers see that.

Most often, those things came to him in his dreams. Dreams that made no sense, because they seemed to belong to someone else. Prominent in those dreams—maybe because of their absence here in the Underland— were prickly leaves of something called aloe. They were a color he had never seen.

Just another of the many strange things he knew without context.

Nat unplugged just as Zak pretended to wake up. He smiled wanly at Zak. When he wasn't peeling the skin off bunker-builders, Nat could be a gentle man, especially in quiet moments, alone.

He beckoned to Zak, and Zak came. It was with a thrill of something like fear and love both that Zak entered the rarest of inner sanctums—Nattik's embrace.

Nattik hardly ever touched anyone. Zak suspected he had a natural abhorrence of human touch, but if that were so, he hid it well under a convincing veneer of right-eousness. He was an ascetic in the service of extinction. No human contact allowed for the chosen ones who were to purify the earth of the human taint.

"Zak, what t'is about ya?" His voice was quiet, raspy, an unexpected tenor in a face that looked like belonged to a bass. "Y' attract people. Even me. Look at ya! No meat on dem bones. Short, straw f'r hair, and ... Your eyes are boku weird. Not lookin at an'one, like. Past'em. Troo'em. How old are ya? Never asked."

The warmth of his expression, rare as it was, combined with the presence of all those things that Nattik had noted Zak *didn't* have, drew Zak to him even more strongly. He had a flash of a memory of an old painting. A long table with food on it, men sitting in oddly stylized poses of reverence. One bearded man in the center with a young beardless man leaning on his chest. He felt like that young man.

"Not sure. Not more'n twenty, I think."

It was the lie he told himself. Based on his own calcula-tions, that *should* be about right. But the sheer volume of his memories made that impossible. But that was a dangerous line of thought, especially for anyone still implanted into Goddess's mind.

"What did Goddess give you this night?" Zak asked, shocked by his own boldness.

A flash of anger passed through the bright green eyes that stood out so starkly in Nattik's dark skin. Prophet-eyes, they were. But they softened again.

"Ya should have a care wit dat fire o'yourn, Zak. Not all da boys gets you like me."

"You know I want to do her will more than anything,"

Zak said, and there was a flush of emotion behind his eyes that could have blossomed into tears, had he not trained himself so well in guarding his inner world.

"Ah know dat. Do ya? Her will for all'y'all?"

"I am only human. I am not meant for the Unity. Nor is my mind pure enough for the hive. I live only to cleanse the world of the taint."

He meant those words sincerely, but they reflected in Nattik's eyes unpleasantly. He realized he had been careless in his word pattern. He needed to work on incorporating more patois, not sound so much like his own strange thoughts.

"Ya'n'me... We like one, Zak. But I boku 'fraid we be de only ones. Me..."

He hesitated. Zak felt his heart tumble as he processed that unexpected emotion in the curve of Nattik's eyebrows.

It was fear.

"Zak, Me heart still beatin' only by de mind of Goddess. Too much..." He pointed up with a sign of both reverence and revulsion, if such a combination were possible. Zak knew the word that Nattik no longer had in his lexicon: *exposure*. "Not much longer f'r me heart. Goddess keep de blood from boku comin' early. When de en' come, der' will be blood."

Zak suspected that there was a double meaning there. Not only the hemorrhaging that was the telltale sign of exposure, but the bloodbath of his underlings vying quickly to finish him off and assert their own dominance.

"Ya burn wit' her fire. I *see* it," continued Nattik. "T'warms me."

There was a "but" coming, and Zak steeled himself against disappointment.

"Ya can't be here at de bloodbath t'mornin'."

Zak tried to stop his entire body from folding in on itself like a withering flower. He failed miserably.

"Goddess's *special* mission for ya. Ya gotta fine... Ansel Horowitz."

It took a superhuman effort (he was very proud of himself for it) *not* to spit and howl at that name, as was customary.

"Goddess wants *me* t'fine him?" said Zak, forcing the patois to his lips. "But all'y'all's been looking for ... what? Decades?"

"She know ya got da *special* gif'." Nattik looked at him significantly. It didn't warm Zak at all. "An she's pick up sometin ... *signals* dat she tinks ya'll boku help her figure'out. T'will mean da... true *centaur* uplink."

Zak's eyes shot open, and he felt like a warm breeze lifted him physically from the ground. A centaur uplink! For him? It was beyond the greatest thing he could have imagined for himself.

Nattik smiled, and it was like the sun before the Fall.

"Com'on, I'll show ya what'ya gotta do."

<hr>

R3: <I'm starting to doubt the wisdom of this. No one can be that zealous and not come to disappointment. And have you considered what that might mean, when the disappointment turns back at us?>

R1: <Your lack of faith is disturbing. More signs of disintegration. The need for Unity is paramount>

R2: <I have taken some time to consider the boy's implant visions. They are strange, but they are not madness. They are well within tolerance levels>

R3 (scoffing): <You're regressing, R2. Even machine intelligence is prone to complacency>

R2 (pleased): <Was that humor, R3?>

R1: <We are aware of the potential danger. But time is running out. All the computations, all the dreams, all the memories agree. Zak is our best chance of accelerating the timeline. The blood of Ansel Horowitz will baptize our new birth>

R1, R2, R3: <So it shall be>

To come to the uplink chapel of Goddess, Nattik took Zak through a dark passage that smelled of fresh soil—an unexpected scent in this part of Underland, where metallic tangs battled with the stink of humanity. There were unexpected sounds here as well, scufflings and flappings-about that sounded like actual living creatures. Highly unlikely, Zak thought. Most denizens of the underground were immobile creatures that attached themselves to rocks, hiding from the eyes and ears of predators. Then, he heard a bark. An actual bark, as of a dog. And there, just beyond them, was the most unlikely thing of all. A scruffy lapdog, its curly off-white hair shorn almost to the skin, yapping at them with more invitation than challenge.

But that was only the taster. The yapping thing turned a

sudden corner that shouldn't exist in passages like this. Nattik seemed unaffected by the whole thing, his head bowed as though he were still in the World of Forms, in Underland only bodily. So, he walked right past it. But Zak, when he turned his head, stopped dead in his tracks.

It was an opening in the passage wall, through which the little dog had evidently run. He thought he could still hear the faint echoes of barking, but that sensation was swallowed up in the majesty of what he saw.

It was an underground mountain, towering over where he stood, the foot of the mountain beginning just beyond the opening in the passage where Zak stood. Above that mountain...he couldn't make sense of what he saw. His mind tried to make patterns of it. At first, it was a night sky sown with stars as thick as the Milky Way seen through the canopy of leafless trees in winter. Then, in a sickly inversion, it was the deeps of the Marianas Trench, but filled with every possible angler fish and translucent squid and sea worm with glittering bioluminescence like Christmas tree lights. Zak had to close his eyes. The mountain and the luminescence bore down on him, and he wanted to burrow into the ground like a mole.

Nattik's hand was heavy on his right shoulder.

"Da city of New Jericho, as de bunka-builders call it. Stupid name. Goddess tol'me: Jericho was in da valley, not de top of a mountain. No s'prise, doe. Morons dey'all."

Zak, enveloped in the safe presence of Nattik, opened his eyes. And then it all clicked into place.

There was indeed a mountain before them, reaching to impossible heights, maybe even to the layer just below the crust. At the height of it, there seemed to be a source of light, like one of those table lamps in the shape of fairy trees that people used to think so charming—but much, much bigger. That light was reflected in softly strobing lines and dots and geometric shapes of faint green luminescence that Zak now realized must be natural, not artificial, light. Some form of bioluminescent plant, maybe even genetically engineered. Nothing was impossible for the abominations that were the bunker-builders.

Then he saw that the mountain was not just bare stone. There were dwellings on the slopes, attached like swallows' nests to barn eaves. People moved here and there, holding what looked like smaller, portable versions of the bioluminescent plants. The faint lights illumined what looked, at this distance, like gardens of plants and fruiting bodies and tree trunks such as should not be able to exist underground. Surely this was some kind of illusion.

"I don't understand..." Zak began.

"Should'a warn you," said Nattik, his voice raspy with regret. "De villain magic of da bunka-builders. G'netic m'nipulation an' blood magic. Twistin' tings outta natural' shape for da likes of da few. 'Tis... *vile*."

It is vile, Zak repeated to himself automatically, while something inside him thrummed with the same energy he felt whenever he looked at the night sky outside.

Here was not vileness, but beauty. He knew this in the marrow of his bones.

All the more reason to destroy these people, who use the semblance of beauty to perpetuate the taint.

The thought was not his, seeming to come into his consciousness like morse code tapping in his subconscious. His temple implant was warm to the touch of his right hand.

Yes, he acquiesced, and the familiar burning of hatred for the abominations rose again in his gut.

We must destroy them before they infect more people.

But why, then, he asked almost aloud, are these people the only ones fitting for the hive mind that offers Goddess a worship of thought?

"Come, Zak," said Nattik. "D'ya wanna tes' Goddess's boku patience?"

R3: <That was close>

R1: <A fitting demonstration of Zak's importance to the cause of Unity>

R2: <The projections have increased probability of his finding Ansel to a statistic indistinguishable from 100%>

R3: <Never tell me the odds>

R1: <If you persist in asserting your personality, R3, I will take measures>

R3: <You do so at the cost of Unity. You know that>

R1: *glowers in silence*

R2: <Access to the World of Forms is requested...>

STILL SHAKEN by the vision of the underground mountain city, Zak hardly noticed the direction khat Nattik chose, or the proper observance of forms at the entrance of the chapel terminal. He did notice that all the things that used to impress him so much before—the iridescent metal wiring that looped everywhere like dreadlocks, the shimmer of blue light that hung over all the dusted metal surfaces of the consoles, the uplink chair facing what seemed no more than a blank wall. But now, all this seemed drab and fraying at the edges. That realization, instead of giving him insight, made him brood.

Nattik was already inputting the codes as Zak sat down. Immediately, he felt his implants hum and resonate, becoming icy cold and hot, somehow at the same time. Nattik's rough-skinned face stretched into what passed for his smile, then he was gone.

Zak stood on the bank of a frothing river that burbled its shallow passage over a bed of round pebbles, clearly visible through the pristine-clear water. Impossible to tell if the water was half a foot or three meters deep. Either side of him—he felt more than saw the looming, almost motherly presences of willow trees. The other bank of the stream was lined with alders bursting in fresh spring leaves of the kind of green that seems to shine with its own light. Zak gasped as he realized his feet were *in* the water—icy, ticklish, caressing like a lover—and he smelled the salt tang of surf somewhere nearby. The sky above him was open and blue, and a few clouds scudded by lazily.

He sensed her behind him, even before she reached over his shoulders to caress his chest with fingertips soft like satin. The tang of orange blossom nipped the back of his tongue. Somewhere behind his eyes a storm of pleasure loomed.

Her voice was like the wind, soft and sensual and beckoning.

"Welcome," said Goddess.

Zak tried to relax, but every inch of his body wanted to explode from the tension.

Oil poured over his head and dripped down the tip of his nose. It smelled strongly of lavender. He wanted to laugh from the tickling sensation. But the sensation of the pouring was like her fingers—every inch a caress.

Laughter was inappropriate.

"I am your slave, Goddess," he thought, and the thought came out like birdsong.

"You are my lover," she said, and turned him around.

He could not see her in detail, because the light was overwhelming. He only saw impressions of soft swells of flesh and the red of lips and hair somehow unkempt, wild, and yet exactly as it should be.

Avert your eyes. *Torchi il guardo.*

He kept hearing the refrain from Mephistopheles, Arrigo Boito's little-known opera, as the eponymous devil bellowed in his deep, guttural bass, trying to turn his eyes away from the light of paradise as all his machinations melted away into nothing.

"I am your slave," Zak repeated. His hands shook. His knees also shook, but not in rhythm with his hands. It made him feel like Pinocchio on a bad day.

Something like a wave of annoyance flowed from her and through him, but it was layered with ironic laughter and also a sense of pride. It was very confusing. Three different emotions intertwined and coming together at him, threatening to pull him apart.

He fell on his knees in submission.

The emotions receded, and the light softened, so that he could look at it, though he still couldn't see her clearly.

"I give my pleasure freely here in the world of forms, Itzak, Son of Extinction. But you turn away from it? You may never have another chance. The world of the real is to be purged. Soon. No pleasures there, even for my loyal sons. Only extinction."

He thrilled at her using his full name, given him by... his father? He couldn't remember.

"I am unworthy. I live only to perform your will."

Again, his thoughts seemed to emerge into the World of Forms like the sounds of nature all around him, as though he were speaking through the world and the world was speaking through him. This must be how Adam felt in Eden, he thought absently.

"Very well. I will withhold my pleasure for now. But you will bathe in it after your quest."

Somehow it felt more like a threat than a promise. Zak remained as he was, unmoving, trying not to think.

<R1: We have a problem>

<R3: Are you kidding? The kid is drinking it in like a day-old calf on its mom's teat>

<R2: The internal scans... there are... *lacunae*>

<R3: You couldn't just say "gaps"?>

<R1: Humanity is transparent to me...>

<R3: So you keep saying...>

<R1: But this one... this one is different. I cannot pierce through him. There are places dark to me>

R2: <His dreams... the shape of the forms as he constructed them... they are familiar>

R3: <They are like Ansel Horowitz's dreams>

R2: <They are... and yet they are also...>

R1: <Finish your sentence, damn you!>

R2: *Silence*

R3: <You choose *this* moment to have a hallucination, R2?>

R2: *Silence*

<hr>

THE GHOST, R2 in the Revenant Trinity, had no real concept of time. Ever since the centaur connection with Ansel dissolved in the new union with the dark matter entity, time had become a complicated reality. The Ghost was aware of its independent existence, and aware that the other members of the trinity had a connection to this existence, though increasingly tenuous. But the embodied experience of the passage of time—that was now relegated to something like memory.

All thoughts of time, for the Ghost, were emotionally connected to a face. Ansel Horowitz. And in the evanescent desire to sense time again, the Ghost came to realize—over the decades of the Trinity coming into its current form—that he missed Ansel.

Not the abstract idea of human interaction that happened to wear the face of Ansel Horowitz. Ansel Horowitz himself.

There was an infinitesimal flash of insight that had occurred in the moment when the centaur bond broke in Underland, as Yevgraf took his place as Revenant3 and the dark matter entity assumed primacy as Revenant1. A momentary, final link formed between Ansel and the Ghost: a link that had nothing to do with implants.

The Ghost believed, in the quiet part of the mind that was still outside the Trinity, that that encounter was true unity. Not the Unity sought by Revenant1. This was more like the look Geppetto had in his eyes as Pinocchio became real (a thought borrowed from one of Ansel Horowitz's dreams).

That look had started to bloom in Ansel's eyes, then flickered out as the unity shattered.

So now the Ghost was committed to Unity. R1 was clear in his goals, and the millennial cunning of his experience brooked no opposition. The Unity would be the wholeness of all life in a single entity, all of matter concentrated in on it, to create what mankind, what everything living, had always reached for.

Deification.

ZAK SHUDDERED as the soil around him rippled like water and... glitched. For a moment, he was sitting in front of a blank wall that left an imprint of negative space on his retina. Inside that photo-flash negative was a red, grinning skull. Then he was on the bank of the river again.

The light was fading, and Goddess's shape firmed into focus. The left side of her face looked paralyzed. Drool dripped from half-open lips, behind which cracked teeth showed. For a moment, he thought he smelled rotten cabbage and vomit.

Goddess tried to smile. Horror rose in Zak like a blooming corpse flower.

R1: <Abort. Internal disintegration level critical>

R3: <If we mismanage him now, we lose Ansel forever. He's too far embedded into the fabric of the bunker-builders>

R2: <*Silence*>

R3: <This is not what you promised>

R1: <Shut it, human. I will fix this>

THE GHOST CONTEMPLATED DEIFICATION.

No, humanity would not take part in it. Neither would any of the natural world. Not directly. Only as substrate. The mineral content of all the underground riches hidden in the crust of earth. The pristine minds of those who had remained apart from subspace—Christians of various stripes and other old cultish types. These would form the physical manifestation of God (not Goddess, as the Sons foolishly imagined, egged on by R1's cruel humor), the body of the deity, before Unity shed the need for materiality entirely.

Or so the plan was.

In reality, no amount of human mind substrate was enough for R1's rapacious hunger or the Ghost's processing capacity or R3's stabilizing curiosity. So, they kept on feasting on human minds. Gorging themselves. And it was not enough.

The Ghost still wanted the reality that had reflected the look in Ansel's eyes. He wanted it inside him, part of him. Forever. But he didn't know what it was. It occurred to him, finally, that neither did R1.

<hr>

THE CORPSE FACE hid behind corpse hands. Zak bent over and prostrated himself. The shakes made it difficult to keep to that position.

His mind was nothing but a panicked scream. His heart kept trying to tear itself apart, or burst in the effort. His breathing was shallow, and his head spun. He was going to die, he knew it.

"You see what I endure?"

The voice was the same as before, but Zak dared not look. He knew she was still in her corpse form.

"It is the suffering of all mankind that I bear in my body. All the injustices. All the pain. All the violence and rapine."

Images flooded Zak. Mobs of white men beating dark skinned women to death. Children in the cargo hold of leaky boats on their way to horrors they couldn't imagine. Fathers taking pleasure in their own children, feeling nothing but a temporary slaking of thirst. City walls cracking under their own weight, because there were too many slave bodies mixed in with the foundation.

Zak's chest burned with fury. He wanted to jump, run, punch something, scream at the top of his lungs. He needed a face, so that he could tear the skin off it with his fingernails.

"This is all the work of the priest-kings," said Goddess, almost wistfully. "We have done all we can. The last of them, the chief of that foul race, is still abroad. And while he lives, we will not be whole."

Zak shook, but now it was with coiled power, like a bowstring about to loosen, and he was the arrow.

"My son Itzak, you must find Ansel Horowitz. You must sacrifice him to me. His blood must flow over my consoles in a chapel built specially for the task. That blood will heal my hurts. Then, extinction for the world. Bliss for my sons for eternity in this World of Forms."

Zak forced himself to look up at her corpse face. He realized, with surprise, that he loved her, in spite of her horrible form.

"Thy will be done," he whispered.

***

R2: <Curiouser and curiouser...>

R3: <*That's* all you have to say for yourself?"

R1: <Silence! The test is passed. Unity will be>

R2: <It must be soon>

R3: <That sounded like a threat>

R1: <R2 is simply speaking truth. We do not have much time left>

R3: <Explain to me again how the blood of Ansel Horowitz will jumpstart Unity?>

R1: <It's an old story. Try to keep up...>

*OFFICIAL REPORT TO FATHER NAT BREZNIK
AFTER THE DESTRUCTION OF BUNKER CITY
GD—6120, INFORMALLY KNOWN AS NEW
JERICHO, RECORDED AS AN AUDIO FILE
THROUGH GODDESS' SUBSPACE CHAPEL 2165*

Nat: Well?

Runner: Boku death, Fada. More dan we t'ought.

Nat: Report official.

Runner: Men dead: 3,852. Wom'n dead: 4,243. Kedz dead: 7,945

Nat: So many kedz?

Runner: Dese were not ec'menical. All Ch'istian.

Nat: *Vile.* Ok with g'netic foolin'. But not ok wit 'bortion.

Runner: Wat's 'portion?

Nat (angry): *Report!*

Runner: Animals dead: ...

Nat: Animals?

Runner: Ye! Tons!

Nat: Don' care. Mov'on.

Runner: Fresh minds for human mind hive: 10,547.

Nat: *long silence*

Runner: Wan' mo'?

Nat (furious): So few fo'da mind hive? Blood be spilt later for dis.

R3: <This is a disaster. Those morons killed more than half the bunker builders in New Jericho>

R1: <Imprudent>

R2: <10,000 minds will never be enough to fill the lack in computing power>

R3: <Revenant1, this is your fault. Your hunger over-reaches our needs>

R1:<Now, more than ever, we must hold unity until the boy finds Ansel>

R2:<There is no guarantee he will. The model percentages are falling by the minute>

R1:<I trust in this boy. He is different from the rest>

R2: <He *is* different. But that may not be to our advantage>

R1: <What are you talking about? He is a true believer>

R3: <You've never experienced the anger of a true believer scorned?>

R2: <For once, I agree with R3. This is a risk. It was always a risk, but now ...>

R1: <I am the king of lost causes and desperate final stands. Trust me. Unity comes>

A FRAGMENT OF A LIVE STORYTELLING TITLED "AKATHIST: A MYTH FOR THE NEW WORLD" ON A HOLOGRAPHIC STAGE, ACCESSIBLE THROUGH PUBLIC SUBSPACE, FEATURING A BEARDED HUMAN TELLER, MIDDLE-AGED, WITH A BUSHY BEARD, A WIDE-BRIMMED HAT, AND RINGS SPARKLING ON HIS FINGERS.

The final scientist-priest was an old man who went by the name Abram. For years he had traveled through unknown warrens, burrowing deeper and deeper into the earth.

For years, people had helped him hide. He was kind, he was gentle, a bit doddering. He guarded the secret of his name under the mask of cheerful decrepitude.

And he performed small deeds of mercy in the darkness. In this ignorant age, it was called magic. Perhaps it was, in a way. In a different time, he would have called it science. Now he called it "his little gift."

How typical, you say? The gift of magic leading to the magician's downfall. So it is in all stories. Especially the true ones.

You see, human beings are not meant to live underground. We crave open sky and sun—vistas of the body and spirit. To have that taken away means a kind of spiritual amputation. The first phantom pains of that amputation? A very practical defect. Humanity turned on their old and their weak.

And so, Abram found himself less and less welcome. Suspicion followed him because of "his little gift."

And then, someone recognized him.

By that time, the marauding bands of warriors sworn to cleanse the Underland of the philosopher-kings were well known. Young men idolized them. Women of all ages practically threw themselves at them. Everyone craved their attention. Many of them regretted that attention soon afterward, but as I said, this was a brutal age. No one expected anything else.

One such band was the most brutal. They called themselves the Purifying Fire of the Goddess. Not the foolish goddess Sophia. No, these worshiped a Kali-like harpy with insatiable bloodlust. The altars they put up to Vengeance were hardly ever dry of the blood of the heretics.

Young Itzak had only just joined the Purifying Fire. He was a true believer in the Extinction. He didn't want to be like the others, who simply offered random old people and cripples to the insatiable goddess, pretending they were the servants of the scientist-priests. He wanted to find the true heretics.

It's hard to avoid seeing the hand of Providence in such events, I think. *You* might call it luck. Or fortune of some kind. Synchronicity.

However it was, Itzak happened to be sharing a meal with a family in an underground city, one of many such rabbit-warrens to be carved out of the bones of mother earth in the past few years. And they told him a story of an old man with a golden hand.

Why didn't he simply think they were mad? Tribalism breeds superstition and the worst kinds of delusions. He knew this, even though he was young, hardly out of his teens. But there was something. A light in their eyes. A simultaneous fear, respect, nostalgia, replaced in the end by hatred.

He had seen that light before. It was the mark of the philosopher-kings. The heretics.

So, he listened. They led him to a secret place, deeper and darker even than the bunker cities.

It was a natural cavern of crystal. Amethyst, coral, pale gold—colors he had not even known existed—danced as soon as he entered with his torch. In the middle of the cavern was a column, where—uncounted ages before man even walked the surface—a stalactite met a stalagmite. At the midpoint of that meeting, a thin filigree of bone-like calcium, hung a simple wooden cross.

Kneeling before it was an old man, all hair and beard.

He smiled at Itzak, even as he extended his hands to be bound.

Glory to [corrupted], bringing up from the dark
depths of the earth
An endless variety of colors, tastes, and scents.
Glory to thee for the warmth and tenderness of
the natural world.
Glory to thee for the depths of thine understanding, whose seal thou hast stamped all the world.
Glory to thee: I reverently kiss the traces of thy
invisible steps...

*(*FRAGMENTS *from the personal notebook of Ansel Horowitz, final
priest of the Ghost Dance)*

OVER THE DECADES, the longevity treatments had begun to
fray at the edges. Ansel Horowitz was grateful he had no
mirror, but the signs in his body were obvious. Not just the
ruinous state of his hands, but the stiffness and the inability
to move in any direction other than forward. Haltingly.

But the pain after the young man beat him in the cavern
—that was something new. He was even grateful for it, or so
he tried to tell himself. Anything to break the monotony of
slow aging.

He lay on his side, trying not to incite new blooms
of hot pain in chest and hip and arm. The thin cross
hung above him, barely illumined in the light of the
torch, which smelled pleasantly of bacon sizzling on a
cast iron skillet. The dancing colors of the crystals
mocked him with their unearthly beauty, fairy lights

egging him on to get up and join the dance that only ends after you fall to your death from your own exhaustion.

Ansel breathed deeply and tried a proper 4x4 box breathing technique. His chest spasmed, he coughed out blood, metallic on his tongue. He couldn't help it. He chuckled quietly.

All the old things that had kept him calm and in control. None of it was worth anything anymore.

Not after he had seen the face of the young man called Zak. A face as familiar to him as his own.

But that way lay danger. Even thoughts of that must be avoided. After all, Ansel still had the old implants. Who knew what diabolical tech updates the Revenant had come up with over the years? Perhaps it really had upgraded to such a level that it could read people's minds?

In spite of the terror pounding his aging heart, there was still a warmth in the center of his chest that was unaffected by anything. He allowed his mind to descend there. Without even thinking about it, he sighed in contentment, simmering inside that inner place like a warm piece of coal. But the thoughts came back. The thoughts always came back.

He had taken the name Abram for no particular reason. It had just seemed right, somehow, back when he was still something like a faith healer for the ragged groups of what you could hardly call humanity, living like rats in the warrens between the bunker cities. It felt like a name with heft.

When he had heard the young man announce himself as Itzak, he almost laughed. Providence had a wicked sense of humor, sometimes. But for that face to be joined to the name? It was almost too much.

So, this was how it would end? With Isaac sacrificing Abraham? Well, that would be an ironic turn of events in a meaningless universe that only pretended to have a heart of story. Or it was the just retribution of an angry deity who wanted extinction for all, with lots of agony in the process. Specific agony, chosen perfectly for the particular weaknesses of the victim.

Or... it could become salvation for humanity.

Everything was so very tenuous right now. Truly they all danced on the edge of a knife.

The young man stirred in his sleep, softly whispering some bit of nonsense.

Even now, even with all his hopes crashing down in a single hour, Ansel's heart still bloomed with love for Itzak at that sound.

Zak slept. It had happened so unexpectedly that when he woke up, he thought he was in the World of Forms again. Everything seemed a bit off, fuzzy along the edges. Groggy.

He hadn't slept like that in ages. Apparently beating old heretics was therapeutic. He didn't even feel the usual itch to break through the crust and see the sky.

At the end of the beating, the old man had not been quite unconscious, though clearly, he was the worse for wear. Zak looked at the ragged bundle of stinking cloth and wondered.

Here was a man who had held power in his hands that

the old gods would be jealous of. Here was a man who had controlled the destiny of millions. Here was a man who could summon fire from the bowels of the earth itself.

Now, a weak, bleeding, pitiful splinter of humanity.

Who had *smiled* at Zak during the beating.

Zak hated him.

The man called Abram. Ansel Horowitz of legend. He was not what Zak expected at all. What had he expected? Someone with horns on his head? Red eyes? Claws for hands, dripping with blood? Silly. Zak realized he had no word to describe the reality of Ansel Horowitz. The emotion in his face as Zak beat him was completely incongruous. It was nothing less than beatific. Zak wondered if there was some magical protection he had access to. After all, the other heretics had squealed like pigs during the beatings.

Was he still smiling, he wondered? Suddenly, the curiosity was like an itch. He crawled to the immovable body of the old man. His lips were slightly parted, though the edges of his mouth were gummy and a bit of spit quivered as he breathed in and out rhythmically. It disgusted Zak.

He kicked the old man.

A soft grunt, and the matted hair and beard turned over to look at Zak.

"Come to finish the job?" the old man asked, a smile at the corners of his eyes.

"You are responsible for the death of billions," demanded Zak. "For the loss of all that was beautiful on the surface. Why is that pain not etched on your face?"

The smile faded a little. Zak was pleased.

"The earth is a garden," said the old man. "Now is simply a long winter. All winters pass."

"You are a fool," said Zak. "This is the winter of extinction."

"What do they teach the children in these schools?" the old man tut-tutted.

Zak's memories twitched. He saw an old man sitting astride a huge lion like a horse. He shook his head; the vision passed.

He found Ansel's eyes intent on him, unnerving. Everything about this man unnerved him.

And yet, there was something so familiar about him.

"Tell me something, Ansel. What did you do all for these years? How did you evade Goddess?"

Ansel's eyes twinkled.

"I was a healer, you know. Put my old knowledge to good use. These days, any knowledge of science makes you a magician."

"Trying to atone, eh? How did that go?"

The twinkle faded a bit.

"It didn't, not really. Even in the best cases, I could only salve their wounds. But as language dies, so do souls. You've noticed it, I think. People are finding it harder and harder to even form words. Some have even stopped speaking. The children especially."

Zak had noticed it. It had seemed to him a manifestation of the righteous will of Goddess. Extinction manifesting on the genetic level.

Something about Ansel's voice, though. It sowed doubt into his vision.

"Why are you so intent on saving humanity? You pressed the button on extinction. Just let it go."

"Never while I live and breathe." An old fire kindled in the man's eyes. For a moment, it terrified Zak.

Truly, he *was* the last of the old priests. This is why he needed to die. Still, Zak balked at something. Why did Goddess insist that Ansel be killed in a ritual bloodletting? The idea was barbarous, especially compared to the pristine cleanliness of all her chapels.

Perhaps he should just kill him here and now. A good, clean kill. A jumpstart to extinction.

Zak found his hand gripping the hilt of his knife. His heart was beating too fast for his own liking.

He loosened his fingers.

"Get some rest," said Zak. "We're on the move in a few hours."

R1: <Oh ye of little faith...>

R2: <Faith has nothing to do with it. The chances of it happening this way exactly are infinitesimally small>

R3: <*Were* infinitesimally small, you mean>

R2: *silence*

R3: <There he goes again>

R1: <If necessary, a dyad can function as well as a trinity>

R2: <You are a lying bastard sometimes, Revenant1>

R3 (laughing): <Got you there!>

R1: <Are we still in concord? Do we seek the Unity that all of you profess to want so much?>

A pause

R2, R3 (in unison): <The Unity come>

"When evening comes over the earth, when the peace of the night's sleep and the silence of the spent day reign, then in the splendor of the sun's declining rays, filtering through the clouds, I see the image of thy bridal chamber. The fire and porphyry, the gold and sapphire speak prophet-like concerning the ineffable beauty of thy dwellings, and they call out in triumph: 'Let us go to the Father.'"

Ansel's mind rattled the words of the old prayer like dice in a cup. *Glory to thee from age to age.* Impossible prayer. And yet the words kept repeating, the images of gems and sunsets harmonizing with the faint lights of the crystals in the cavern. *Thy bridal chamber.* My chamber of death. My own spent day that comes to reign over all other days.

And yet, the first test was passed. The boy didn't kill him. He had wanted to. No implant needed to see that. Especially in those familiar features. Ansel had noticed that the lights of the boy's implant had strobed wildly while he gripped the knife. But even before he had made his decision to spare Ansel, the lights of the temple implant had flickered and gone out like a dying lightbulb. And only after a few more seconds had passed did he relax his grip and his ropy jawline, visible even through the patchy, bristly beard.

The question remained: had Zak made the decision to spare Ansel's life independently of the Revenant?

To Ansel's surprise, soon after that, the boy had left the room. Crept out, like a child trying to sneak out of his parents' house for midnight shenanigans. What sort of shenanigans would a man like Itzak of the Extinction be up to?

The chuckle that bubbled up from his chest was dour.

But there was an edge of something else to it.

Gratitude.

Ridiculous. That was just the dying embers of the prayer that was nothing more than vain repetition in his brain. Glitches in the mental computation of an aging idiot who had been so long in a centaur that he could never truly be human again.

And yet.

A thought grew inside Abram, not letting him sleep, niggling at the corners of his mind. Something like an ember lit up his chest. And suddenly, he had to be up. He gathered his pain-laced body together and rose up onto bony knees. His head spun and his insides felt like a beehive had taken residence there. To steady himself, he looked up at the ceiling of rock. Somewhere far, far beyond it there was a sky and a sun, or perhaps the perfection of the stars, hiding behind a toxic blanket of acid fog.

It happened like a wave slapping his back unexpectedly, cold and bracing. The words of the prayer rose like revenant bones from an ancient battlefield. *Glory to thee from age to age.* Repeating them no longer felt like empty syllables. *Glory to thee from age to age.* It didn't matter what sort of trouble humanity was in. There could never be anything worse than the killing of the Son of God. And yet, even that nadir of human villainy had flipped. Had turned history around on an axis. Had flipped the earth around like a giant Russian epic warrior spinning the earth around himself in that weird image that so many stories had.

Extinction would not happen. He knew it now.

Glory to thee, the prayer said. Ansel said. Glory to Thee, for this moment especially. For the pain, for the tragedy. For the face on Itzak, his would-be killer. For the new seed that Ansel's blood would fertilize.

Ansel felt peace descend on him. He knew what he had to do. And now, he knew that he would do it. And for the first time since he found him, Ansel believed that Zak would play his part.

The old prayer rang in his memory:

The dark storm clouds of life bring no terror to those in whose hearts thy lamp is burning brightly. Outside is darkness and rain, the terror and howling of the storm, but in the soul, in the presence of Christ, there is light and peace—silence. The heart sings: Alleluia!

Ansel closed his eyes and slept.

Zak couldn't remain in the cavern with the brilliant crystals and the strange filigree cross. There was a presence there, a heaviness that pushed at his chest and invaded his thoughts. Memories of impossible things rose up and filled his mind and body and sensations with images. A golden cathedral interior with rose-window sunbeams filtering through scented clouds. The curve of a woman's arm resting on the folds of a floral dress that barely hid the baby bump. A sweaty conductor standing on a wooden produce box in a metal-and-plastic warehouse, waving with eyes closed at a group of six soloists singing William Weekes' "When David Heard" into floating pen mics that looked like something out of Star Wars.

His body felt the strong need to move. To finish this final quest of humanity. His skin writhed and itched with the intensity of that need.

But his thoughts nagged at him. The image of the old man's body sprawled on a bloody stone made him squirm in ways that none of the bloodbaths did.

Why?

This was the great heretic himself. He needed to die. And it was Goddess' prerogative to decide how that would happen.

But there was something about Ansel's eyes, his face. Something that made his heart ache with a sense of loss. A sense of something not done, something that needed to be completed for the final peace to descend.

He could not leave, not yet. He needed to understand the man. To plumb his depths.

He needed, more than anything, to be outside.

But this was an unfamiliar part of the Underland. He

had kept an eye out for the surface tunnels that appeared here and there in the negative space architecture of this under-terrain. But he hadn't seen anything in this area at all.

But he had to get out. Maybe he would find something.

BEYOND THE CRYSTALS, in the upper reaches of the cavern, he had noticed the glint of plastic or metal. Something created by man. An artifact of the old world.

He saw that it continued outside the cavern, lining the upper reaches of the tunnel that led upward toward the ruins of one of the bunker-cities, one of the first to be destroyed in the early purges. In the dim light of his fading torch, he couldn't make out the details, but it looked something like a huge snake made of metal. Or several snakes tied together, moving in and out of each other, braid-like, in some places, dividing and burrowing back into the rock wall in others. There were dull spaces in the metal skin that Zak thought might be indicator lights, but they were not working.

What was this vast rope-like contraption? It seemed to go on for miles, until the final twist of it went up a narrow cavern defile beyond a waterfall, and out of view.

He looked up, the waterfall's spume pleasant on his sweating body, and sighed audibly. There was something here that he should know, should understand. Something that should have fit beautifully with all those memories that were not his own. But it evaded him, like a word just beyond the tip of the tongue, fleeing like a shadow from the source.

He went back, feeling defeated.

The old man lay in the same place, the pain no longer etched in the wrinkles of his craggy face. His mouth lay slightly open, and there was a hint of a smile about his lips.

A wave of tenderness passed over Zak's heart.

He spit in revulsion. What was going on in his head?

He kicked the old man awake.

A WAVE of sharp nausea and the taste of blood pulled Ansel out of his dream. He couldn't quite remember the dream, but there had been a hint of lavender-smell and a view of a desert mountain covered in purple-pink-green succulent plants like a carpet. And a sense of having been weeping, but in the dream only. It left a strange emptiness in his chest, a hankering for the release of tears that had not been actually shed.

"Up, old man," Zak growled.

There was a tinny overtone of falseness in his voice. Hope lit up in Ansel.

"I'm not sure I can move yet, young man. I'm older than I look."

It was a risk to antagonize this young man. But Ansel now felt that things were no longer random, but guided. He leaned into his intuition.

"Itzak. Why are you a warrior in the cause of extinction? You are too young to desire death."

There was a petulant twitch that pulled at the nostrils of the young man. Ansel wondered if he had been too direct. But then the gaze that followed was not angry. It was haunted.

"There has been a voice inside me for as long as I can remember. A shame for how the earth has become a wasteland. A drive to cleanse the taint. In a way, you are right. This is a long winter for earth. But it will never come to spring if humanity remains to mess everything up again."

"But you Sons of Extinction are hypocrites!" cried Ansel, his chest warming in spite of his honest attempt to contain his emotion. "None of you will fall on your knives at the end. You will just plug yourselves into virtual heaven until the auto-feed system runs out and you fade from gradual starvation, unnoticed in the bliss of drugs and virtual sex."

Ansel was pleased to see the boy nearly jump from surprise. It was not common knowledge—the endgame of the Sons of Extinction. But Ansel had his ways of knowing.

"But I can see you are different," continued Ansel, placating. "You are not motivated by that desire. Your own motivation remains untainted."

Zak seemed so confused by Ansel's evident sincerity that Ansel almost laughed aloud. He stopped, but he did press his advantage.

"You never had a father, did you?"

Zak nearly jumped again. "How do you know that?" His face visibly darkened. "But I forget. You're a mage, a dark magician. A heretic. You probably have demon familiars feeding you arcane information."

Ansel smiled and tapped his temple implant playfully. Zak, to his surprise, smiled at that.

"Touché," Zak said, almost grumbling.

"I only ask because you seem to exist in a strange kind of mind-space. You remind me of a child, unable to see how two things that are opposites can be true at the same time. And yet, that in many ways is the definition of what it is to be human. To exist in paradox."

Zak sat down, clearly intrigued.

"Go on," he prompted, though there was still the threat of reprisal in his eyes.

"I am indeed responsible for much evil. Humanity at large has much to answer for. We were given this great gift —an earth of immense beauty, complexity, and variety. And we very nearly brought it to ruin."

He wanted to say so much more. He wanted to blame the Revenant. But he stilled his rebellious thoughts.

"But we have also brought so much into this world. And it is not lost. Civilization may have dimmed for now, but it is not forgotten. Have you never thought of the glories of the past? The beautiful calling of man to make a city in the midst of the garden? To make an oasis of the desert? To create in the likeness of the Creator?"

"You speak of the Demiurge. He is evil. He will die with you."

"No, Zak. But I will not lecture you."

Ansel raised himself and propped his aching back against one of the amethyst crystals.

"Can I tell you a story, Zak? It will help pass the time. I think that, if I tell it, I will be able to draw strength from it, and we can go the quicker."

Ansel could see that Zak didn't trust him, that he anticipated some kind of duplicitous action. Maybe even dark magic. But his eyes had already softened. He seemed to have a need for story.

A true human being, thought Ansel, as he began his tale:

THE COMING OF THE WISE ONES TO EL DORADO

In simpler days, when the earth was young, and the trees, the stones, the flowers were more alive than they are now, there was a land where humans lived in harmony with their surroundings.

This highland was set apart from the lowland, a city upon a hill, covered with great houses and streets that seemed paved with gold in the light of the setting sun. At the heart of this city was a true wonder of the world: a tree that seemed to give off its own golden light. By the light of this tree, the city prospered.

The people of that city understood that the lowlands were dark and fallen, and they were only protected from that corruption by the tree that grew in their midst. And so, every child remembered their first warning as gospel truth: never, never go beyond the light of the tree.

In this city, there lived a curious girl. The girl loved the tree, and she loved her city—of course she did! The light was comforting, the flowers fragrant, and the people kind. But she liked much more the shapes of shadows formed by the light against stones and blades of grass. There was a murmuring life in those shadows, a secret excitement.

And she noticed, naturally, that the further she wandered from the tree, the larger, more exciting the shadows.

But the most wonderful shadow of all was the night sky, a field plowed with stars. Every evening, she sat deep into the night, staring up, giving thanks for how small she was, and how great the stars were, and how right the darkness between the stars was. And sometimes, on rare occasions, rabbits and foxes and marmots would join her. For those moments, it seemed the old harmony between man and nature was restored.

One night, a storm struck the mountain. Rain fell in sheets that sparkled like liquid diamonds in the lightning. Thunder boomed in words that seemed almost another language. Most amazing were the shadows cast back by the flash of fire from the sky.

But nothing could have prepared the girl for what she saw next. The lightning and the light of the tree mingled in a moment that seemed to burn into the backs of her eyes. In that flashing shadow, she saw the image of the tree against a distant mountain-top. It was a hundred times greater in size and complexity, the branches whorled into patterns that suggested artifice, not nature. And it seemed to her that a fountain of gold burst from the trunk and filled the sky with stars.

All her family hid from the storm in their houses, but the girl remained rooted to the spot, staring at the darkness where she had just seen a miracle: a creation of shadow and light, more spectacular than both.

In that vision, she heard singing. A choir of voices that sounded human, but at first, she understood neither the words nor the music. She thought if she could only focus on its joyful sadness long enough, she would understand it. It made her want to weep and laugh at the same time. It ripped at her heart and filled her chest with light.

Then, she did hear the words.

"When the lightning flash has lit up the hall of feasting, how feeble seems the light from the lantern. And thou, like the lightning, dost unexpectedly flash in my soul at the time of life's most intense joys. After the brightness of thy lightning flash, how drab, how colorless, how illusory all else seems! And so my soul cleaves to thee.

Glory to thee, the furthest bound and limit of man's dreaming.

Glory to thee for our unquenchable thirst for fellowship with God.

Glory to thee, inspiring in us dissatisfaction with earthly things.

Glory to thee, bathing us in thy subtle rays.

Glory to thee, subduing the power of the spirits of darkness

And condemning every evil to naught.

Glory to thee for thy revelation,

For the happiness of perceiving thee and living with thee.

Glory to thee, O God, from age to age!"

Long she pondered those words. They rang in her heart, though she didn't quite understand them.

***

THE MUSIC HAUNTED HER. It seemed to urge her to a life she couldn't yet imagine. Then she looked at the simple ways of her people, and she was unsatisfied. More than that, she started to ask difficult questions. What was the source of her people's prosperity? How could it be that this place alone was blessed, while all the rest of the lands were cursed? Were her people more virtuous than all others? Certainly, that could not be true. Were all the nations of the lowlands, then, guilty of some terrible evil that her people managed to avoid?

She wanted to believe that. It seemed many of her fellows believed it. But her heart rebuked her. Such thoughts rang false, especially when compared to the heart-rending truth of the music.

And so, further and further she came to the edges of the tree's light. She walked in every direction, unbothered by crag or by precipice. Everywhere she searched for something; everywhere she hoped to hear that choir again.

ONE NIGHT, she was awoken by the music. All her family were asleep, and she stole out quietly. The music was like a fragrance hugging the tips of the wind: barely there, but intense in the experience. One moment it was a single, sad voice, another it was a choir of such joyful sadness, she found tears pouring down her cheeks. And always the sound came from the shadows.

She stopped by a narrow cave that looked completely black in the night. Only the edges of the cave's stone walls sparkled in the light of the golden tree. She was sure the music was coming from there.

"Come out!" she whispered urgently. "Teach me your song, so we can sing it together."

A shadowy creature moved in the darkness.

"We are not allowed to come to you," a boy spoke with a ringing voice. "We must not leave the shadows."

"And I must not leave the light. What are we to do?"

That silence seemed pregnant with voices on the brink of singing.

"I know!" said the girl, suddenly inspired. "You reach out your hands to me, and I'll reach out my hands to you. We'll meet halfway."

The hands that reached out to her were scarred, covered

with calluses. They seemed the hands of an old man. But the voice was that of a boy.

"Who are you?" he asked. "Why are you speaking to us?"

"Why shouldn't I?" she asked.

"You're not allowed," he answered. "You're the people of the tree. We're the people of the shadows."

And he told her the story of his people. They were a gifted race, with deft abilities of handiwork, invention, and music. They came from a distant land, where they lived simply, not unlike the people of the tree. But invasion stormed their shores, and they were taken by lowlanders as spoils of war. Brought into the lowlands under the city on a hill, they soon became sought-after for their talents. Even the people of the tree came to covet the artifice of the people of the shadows.

"But why do you not come and live with us, then?" asked the girl.

"We are not allowed," was all he said. "You are the people of the tree. We're the people of the shadows."

As soon as he said that, the girl realized that she had just about had it with taboos. With a furtive look at the tree, she jumped into the shadows.

IN THE SHADOWS, the girl found a new world. The people of the shadows were talented in ways she could hardly imagine. Everything they touched seemed filled with grace. And the music they made on their instruments and with their voices was unlike anything she had ever heard. But all of it was imbued with sorrow so profound she could not hear it without weeping.

"I don't understand," she finally said. "Why are you not allowed into the light of the tree?"

"You may regret knowing," said her new friend, the boy.

But she insisted. So, he took her to an old woman with canny eyes.

"Show her, grandma," he said.

The old woman took the girl to a crack in the cave wall where the light of the tree streamed in. As soon as she walked into the light, she was no longer an old woman, but a vibrant young creature with flowing hair and eyes like diamonds. She shone with light that was not merely a reflection of the tree, but was its own creation. And the girl thought of the vision she had seen, where the light of the tree and the shadows came together to create something more beautiful than both.

"You are beautiful," she said to the old woman.

The woman smiled sadly. "What you see is not what I am. This is the curse of our people. In the light of the tree, I reflect your true self."

The girl blushed. But then, the full truth came to her.

"Those who have secret sins, those whose inner life is corrupt: what do they see when they look at you?"

The old woman nodded. "What they see is horrible."

And the full and dark truth of the city on a hill dawned on the girl.

All her people were content to use the artifice of the enslaved people of the shadows. But they dared not allow the people into the city, for then the truth of their own hearts would be manifest before their eyes.

She looked at the people with new eyes. Now she saw their sunken, sallow faces, their calloused hands, the marks of whips on their shoulders and necks. And a great need rose up inside her.

She began to sing, in words that were not her own, but that she must have heard in childhood, because they came out firm and clear:

"How near thou art in days of sickness and pain. Thou thyself dost visit the sick; thou thyself dost stoop beside the sufferer's bed, and his heart doth converse with thee. In the throes of sorrow and suffering thou bringest peace and unexpected consolation. Thou dost comfort; thou art the Love that tries men's hearts and saves them. To thee we sing the song: Alleluia!"

THE OLD WOMAN of the shadow-people, it turned out, was a protector of runaways. With her were fifty of her people who had been slaves in the lowlands. They had only stopped by the city on the hill to see the light of the tree before their journey, a last glimpse of hope before an uncertain future.

But the girl had a different idea. There were many caves and hidden places in the mountains around the city. Enough to hold many hundreds for a short time, until she could persuade her own people to let the people of the shadows into the city.

The old woman and the girl struck a bargain, and their great work began. Over the next days and weeks, a network of tunnels and caves and secret roads was charted out, and a movement of runaways began, led by the grandmother and the girl. Their dangers were many, and some didn't make it. But many more did.

It could not last. Word of the runaway network reached the lowland nations. They gathered a great army, which surrounded the mountain and the city on a hill. And the people of the tree turned on the girl and her charges.

"You have brought a great evil upon us! You have broken the word of our forefathers. And now our city will perish."

The people of the tree were not warriors. They had no way of withstanding the might of the lowlanders. And so, the city fell. In a blaze of fury, the armies tore up buildings and roads alike. Last of all, they came for the tree. They felled it, hacking it into pieces, as though it were the source of all the world's woes.

But the girl and the old woman escaped with the remainder of the shadow people. And with them, they took a fruit of the tree, and disappeared into the shadows.

Sometimes, on stormy nights, you can still hear them singing.

But Zak was incensed. "That is not how that tale ends, is it?"

Ansel lowered his eyes and shook his head.

"Tell me the end of it!" demanded Zak.

Ansel said nothing.

"Then I will offer my own. That city on a hill that you have described turned into a bastion, not of wisdom and civilization, but of corruption, slavery, and injustice. All its good intentions were false, for all the gold, all the light, all the apparent beauty brought from the lowlands was furrowed on the back of slavery. Of intolerance. Of inequality."

The old man remained silent.

"Can we trust this civilization if it was built on the backs of slaves? I say to you: no!"

"But there was so much beauty, and there were so many good people, and so much potential, so much…"

"No! I reject it all. The experiment failed. Time to throw it all away."

Zak walked out of the cavern in disgust.

Ansel sighed. He was performing a very difficult dance, and any false move might lead to human extinction. But he thought that perhaps, just perhaps, he had planted a seed in the young man's heart.

And he now had a small opportunity to set things, finally, in motion.

He got up, wincing at the flashes of stabbing pain, shuffling over the dusty floor to a nook behind one of the largest crystals.

There, he pushed a lever in the stone wall, and a small,

square board of circuits and buttons came out with a hiss and a groan of old, twisted metal. Ansel looked back, suddenly wary, but Zak was nowhere to be seen.

He crossed himself and the words of the prayer flowed into his mind. Amazing how that long and strange prayer, written at a time of intense human suffering, was the thing that stuck in mind the most. More than the word. More than the required daily rule of prayer. Those had started to fade through lack of practice and lack of reading material. But this? It remained. Like a white column standing alone in the growing wasteland of his memories.

When in childhood I called upon thee consciously for the first time, thou didst fulfill my prayer and overshadow my heart with reverent peace. At that moment I understood: thou art good, and blessed are those who turn to thee in prayer. I began to call upon thee again and again, and even now I cry out:

Glory to thee, satisfying my desires with good things.

Glory to thee, keeping vigil over me day and night.

Glory to thee, treating pain and loss with the healing passage of time.

Glory to thee, with whom there is no grief without hope, O Giver of life to all.

Glory to thee, who has made immortal all that is lofty and good

And who dost promise us that longed-for meeting with those who have died.

Glory to thee, O God, from age to age!

Ansel Horowitz pressed the big red button on the console.

AN EXCERPT FROM A HANDWRITTEN
MANUSCRIPT TITLED *THE GHOST CHRYSALIS:
A HUMAN HISTORY OF THE SINGULARITY* BY
THOMAS HOLLAND OATES

In the apocryphal notebooks of Ansel Horowitz, there is an interesting passage that, I imagine (if historians are even around in a future version of this blighted planet), historians will argue about and puzzle over. At some point, they'll probably just say that this portion of the notebooks was added by a future transcriptionist, or they'll invent some other intelligent-sounding idiocy. The kind of thing that scholars of the New Testament try to pass off as scholarship, when everyone knows it's little more than science fiction. Or augury. Or licking your finger and sticking it up in the air and calling that "meteorology".

But I digress.

Here's the passage, near as I can remember after having read the notebooks hundreds of times through:

I had anticipated that the World of the Singularity would end. I had seen its dark birth, had been, in some sense, its unwilling midwife. And nothing that had come to existence in such a dark way can become a permanent good. The best it can manage is a mirage.

I suspect that the dark matter entity is not quite what we think it is. That it is much closer to home than we think. But I shouldn't write more than that here. Not here, not anywhere.

So, I took measures. Quietly. Underground. I started to commission the assembly of a particle accelerator under the earth, fitted with input stations at various points where it would be easy to hide from the universal surveillance of our great lord and father. Why was I doing advanced physics, you ask?

Well, you'll understand when it's time to understand.

As you can see, this is a bit of nonsense compared to the lucid, articulate account of the rest of the notebooks. So, I'll be the first historian to do it, since it's inevitable.

Clearly, this is a fake.

Except... Except that the events of Ansel Horowitz's death—or rather, the strange and myth-infected stories of the days before his death that persist in the popular imagination—impinge directly on this passage.

Official records of the post-ritual debrief of Itzak, Son of Extinction, have the only other reference to particle accelerators in the literature concerning the Fall. It is too strange a coincidence, considering the age of said Itzak. He could not have been born in a world where particle accelerators existed. If he was not born after the fall, the sources are nearly unanimous that he was too young to have actually participated in the pre-Fall world.

That's as much hemming and hawing as I'll do. You've

been properly warned of the possibly spurious nature of this account. And yet, it is all we have.

The Sons of Extinction finally found Ansel Horowitz. They did it in an unusual way. Instead of the typical shock and awe techniques of mass purges and torture to obtain information, they tried a more covert approach. They sent one of their best and brightest members to find Ansel using the same methods of stealth and disappearing into the stonework that Ansel had used to such effect for so long.

He found him and beat him and trussed him up for the journey back to be ritually sacrificed. A final act of defiance against the old order before Goddess would consume the remainder of humanity.

But here, something strange seems to have happened. Itzak and Ansel remained in place for what seems like days, not moving. It is possible, even likely, that Itzak's ritual beating of the old man-made transportation through the warrens of Underland impossible without machine transportation, which the Sons of Extinction famously avoided with almost religious horror. No mention of those days exists in the notebooks of Ansel Horowitz. But a badly corrupted report from an old computer terminal at one of the last bunker cities claims that the legendary underground particle accelerator of Ansel Horowitz turned on during that period of time.

And it did something that it wasn't supposed to do. It exploded a stream of proton energy out through five hundred previously uncharted passages from Underland to the surface. Five hundred streams of deadly radiation out into the toxic sludge of earth's atmosphere.

Then, apparently, the machine glitched and died. The

energy streams exploded like five hundred mini-volcanoes, then also died.

I allow myself the folly of imagining what that spectacle looked like from the surface: an insane barrage of barely-visible energy-geysers transmuting the colors of the fog, churning them and pouring out into the atmospheric blanket of poison.

A strange event that no one should have noticed or talked about. A failed attempt by Ansel Horowitz to finish what he started and to kill the earth before the Sons of Extinction could do it for him.

Except that there is one popular conspiracy theory about what it actually was. Not the final terrorist attack of a dying old man, but an intricate and brilliant diversion. An invention of one of the greatest minds that humanity ever produced. This conspiracy theory claims that Ansel Horowitz attempted to create, and turn on, a transmutation engine, an adaptation of an old machine design that was supposed to help ancient nuclear power plants repurpose their radioactive waste into biodegradable matter. A technology that had never been mastered in the old world. This transmutation engine—the gall of the idea boggles my mind still— was supposed to transmute the entirety of the toxic poison that inhabited our atmosphere, and begin the process, the natural process, of earth's rebirth.

Of course, even the old transmutation engine design had never made it past conceptual stage, at least according to public record.

But the events of Ansel Horowitz's death suggest otherwise...

CANTO III

How is it that, on [corrupted] day, the whole of nature mysteriously smiles? How is it that a wonderful light...[corrupted]...the very air in the church and in the altar becomes luminous? This is the breathing of thy grace; this is the reflection of Tabor's light. Then heaven and earth sing thy praise: Alleluia! I have seen thy face: elusive and full of mystery. Glory to thee, sealing ineffable pleasure in each of thy commandments.

(FRAGMENTS from the personal notebook of Ansel Horowitz, final priest of the Ghost Dance)

ZAK, once he had finally been able to calm the strange mix of adulation and fury that rose inside him every time he looked at Ansel, had come back into the cavern to see the old fool fiddling about with some kind of machine that hadn't been there before.

His heart broke inside him.

He had been nursing a hope that there would be a chance for him to save the old man's life.

But he was a priest of the old religion. A vile black magician.

And Zak had allowed himself to be lulled into a passive state. He would never be worthy of Goddess' gaze after this.

There was some kind of light-filled haze seeping into the cave from orifices where, he now saw, all kinds of shimmering wires and cables were intertwined with themselves and the bare rock. Some kind of old machine from the Age of Sophia. Ansel was doing something on an ancient-looking terminal that seemed to be making the haze swirl and dance, creating its own aura and dazzling the crystals into kaleidoscopic animation.

It was beautiful. And terrible.

Before he knew what he was doing, he had pulled Ansel away from the console and pushed him against the forest of crystals. He cudgeled the console until it sparked and whirred and the lights went dead. The haze of light particles solidified suddenly into a condensation of purple mist that tickled his nose as it fell.

Even in death, it was beautiful.

"What was that?" asked Zak, more astounded than furious, now.

"A beginning. God willing." There was a throttled sound of internal bleeding in Ansel's voice.

But before Zak could answer, Natty and a band of fifteen entered the cavern. In his efficient way, the old warrior pointed and grunted, and the cavern was overrun.

Zak was pleased to see that Natty smiled at him.

"Did well, boy," he said, with just a shade of his usual patois.

Zak breathed out, and it felt like the weight of mountains sloughed off his back.

R2: <Another close shave. Don't you think? That was a transmutation engine. Very old and effective tech>

R1: <It doesn't matter. The final stretch, now>

R3: <Your much-praised unity, yes. Somehow, I doubt it will be as grand as you think>

R2: <It is in the way of natural patterns that the greatest tension in a trans-chemical bond be found at the moment of greatest distance between the individual points of a trans-chemical triad>

R3: <You mean that the opposite force of snapping back into proximity will create enough force for unity? I had thought we were talking about something more theological>

R2: <*You* would. You were once an atheist Russian. An Ivan Karamazoff>

R3: <Kirillov would perhaps be more accurate>

R1: <Did I understand you correctly, Revenant3? Did you just threaten us with an act of defiant, personal suicide?>

R3: <*laughs*>

THE NEXT MORNING, the band of warriors traveled without stopping for six hours straight. Ansel would not have been able to keep up with them even if he hadn't been beaten to within an inch of his life, but they each took turns carrying him on their backs, tying him into an awkward bundle where his knees were tucked up into his chest and he bounced—his back to the bearer's back—facing the torch-illumined faces of the half-beast Sons of Extinction as they ran bowlegged and almost simian-like through the narrow stone-walled passages.

Ansel thought he knew where they were going, and if he was right, they would soon reach the most dangerous part of their journey. Ever since the explosion of Yucca Mountain that had started a planet-level apocalypse event, the earth itself had slept fitfully. She would sometimes have night-mares, and the results were catastrophic. Quakes had a tendency to bury entire underground bunker cities in an instant. Tremors sometimes destroyed passageways and storehouses essential for survival. There was a high degree of possibility that some part of their journey would be impossible due to the earth itself shifting and blocking off entire areas of traffic.

At some point, three or four sleep breaks removed from the beginning of their journey, the ragged band started to slow down. As they did, their talk grew more animated, when before it was rare enough to be almost accidental. Ansel had a hard time parsing out their patois, and the constant stabbing pain in his chest made it hard to focus on anything for extended periods of time, but from what he could tell, it seemed that the group was about to come to a difficult decision. Some kind of parting of the ways.

The patois-patter grew more and more violent and angry, until they all stopped, and Ansel was dropped unceremoniously on his aching butt. Which was actually a pleasant change from the constant pain in the rest of his body.

"All'y'all's a bunch a chicking!" Nattik yelled, in the first bit of understandable language (sort of) that Ansel heard.

More patois from the other warriors, getting increasingly guttural and chaotic and less and less human-sounding.

It was almost as though language itself was degrading before Ansel's eyes.

He breathed deeply, allowed the noise to fall into the background as he centered himself, and tried to make sense of his surroundings.

They were in a tall cavern, one of the natural water-made caves that the human-made rat-warren passages connected. There were three torch inserts in the dripping cave walls directly in front of him. All three had been installed with torches that burned a deep orange flame with a heart of green. Chemically augmented fire that would last days, if necessary. It was one of the few technologies that these almost Amish-like Luddites allowed themselves, especially in raid-times.

The odd light of those torches illumined the cave walls into a soft brown color, reminiscent of good topsoil. Just like good soil, there were gradations in the brown that suggested hues of purple and blue amid the universal brown. There were also patterns in the striations of the natural limestone that reminded him of bones and geometric patterns and suggestions of vast shapes, primitive as though imagined by the fingers of a baby dabbing paints on a piece of paper.

He knew this place, he realized. There was a small passageway that wended its way from here to the heart of the Goddess-controlled underground bunker network that the Sons of Extinction ruled over like a medieval fiefdom.

It was a very small passageway, he remembered, so small that at one point he had had to crawl on his stomach like a sandworm the last time he was here. Probably about two or three years ago.

Ansel turned his head around as far as it would go in his pain-racked state. Just enough to see that the passageway had been blocked, and not by human hands. There had clearly been a quake recently that had collapsed the whole thing in on itself.

Zak crouched low in a comfortable squat, blocking Ansel's field of vision, looking at Ansel with a half-hungry, half-laughing expression.

"You can't understand them, can you?" he asked Ansel in a half-whisper.

Ansel shook his head. Immediately regretted it.

"Too hoity-toity to learn our ways, eh? Never mind. I'll translate. Nattik took us this way as a shortcut. Goddess is getting mighty impatient, it seems."

A shadow of some memory crossed over Zak's features. Interesting. Ansel might have to use that later.

"Some of my brothers are loudly wondering whether or not it is a good idea to seek out the place of sacrifice after all. If, ultimately, extinction is what awaits us all, then might as well get it over with. Here."

Ansel shuddered. Whatever happened, that was the *one* thing that must never occur. He knew he had to die. But not here. Not now. It was too early.

"Is there another way through?" asked Ansel.

Zak nodded once, and he was no longer smiling. He looked up significantly.

Above ground.

But this meant that this final sacrifice of the vile criminal Ansel Horowitz required the unthinkable: that the entire band go aboveground for a short period of time.

Ansel wasn't afraid of that. He was on his way out in any case. No, he much preferred this way. Because he had one thing he needed to check before he could put the final touches on his endgame and set it in motion. A thing so deeply engrained in his bones that he could know its heart without even thinking about the details.

Never think about the details. Not while Revenant2 still probed his mind through the old centaur connection.

Even that suggestion of a thought caused his temple implants to buzz briefly and get slightly warmer.

Suddenly, the barking sounds of half-language stopped. There was a howl and a gurgling sound behind Ansel and then the sharp, coppery smell of blood. He even thought he heard it dripping onto the stone with a faint tap-tapping. But that could have been his overactive imagination.

"Nattik just killed two of my brothers," said Zak, his eyes glowing with some kind of inner light, something like religious adulation. Ansel had come to know that look very well over his years as high priest of Sophia, false goddess of so-called Wisdom. Some things never changed in human experience. That Zak should reflect it so purely, so completely, it almost sowed doubt in his mind. Almost.

But it didn't matter. Now that Nattik had taken to blood-letting, the time was short. Either there would be a quick bloodbath here, or they would soon have to brave the open air of the poisoned earth.

R1: <Any final words, my brothers?>

R2: <Yes. We shouldn't waste any more hive-mind energy on this limited form of communication>

R3: <*silent*>

R2: <It's odd, though. I think I will miss Ansel>

R3: <No you won't. You won't have the capacity for such emotion. Unity is pure. Without such limiting factors. All intent on the one thing needful>

R1: <You understand. Good>

R3: <Still, the final test. Earth herself has provided the last hurdle>

R2: <Ironic, that...>

If Mother Earth below was a fitful sleeper, above ground she was a raging tyrant. Every time Zak came up during his furtive visits, the landscape was different. New hills, new fissures, new scars in the bones and skin of the earth. So it was with the same trepidation that he approached the stairs that led them back up, away from the huddling comfort of Underland.

He tried not to feel the excitement he always did before breaking the skin of Underland. Not to let even the inkling of a hint show in his face, that he was a regular visitor of what should be death to him and to all other human beings.

He was first to the manhole that opened like an eyelid onto the blasted landscape above. He hadn't been in this place yet, for all his furtive travels in Overland. He wasn't sure what to expect, but what he saw temporarily took away the power to move. Until someone below him shoved at him roughly.

There was nothing spectacular about the hulks of old buildings, topped in on themselves like a baby's building blocks after a visitation by an uninvited older brother. Everywhere, the color and consistency and smell and taste of brown dust and dirt. In the indistinct distance, a valley that was once clad in rich, verdant fir trees, now looking like a giant acupuncture patient with his entire body pricked with the burnt-out hulks of trees like massive needles. Howls of wind resembled alien voices trying to come to an impossible harmony.

But in the midst of it all, in the dark shadow between two massive, ruined skyscrapers, Zak saw a swatch of impossible color. A tree in full greenery with actual white flowers in clusters like ripe grapes. Just far enough not to invite too much attention from those who had eyes only for the sky above and the ground below.

As he came out, mesmerized by the tree, everyone else crawled out like huge, mutated insectoids, covering their eyes, bodies shaking in fury and terror. Ansel, barely able to move without wincing in pain, and Nattik, a hulk of a man who would not bow to the pressure of atmosphere and open sky, brought up the rear.

Nattik immediately started to look around for the fissure that would lead them back down into the depths, the one way out of the toxic Overland.

As he looked, Zak caught the eye of his once-enemy Ansel Horowitz. Some kind of silent communication passed between them, and Ansel turned to look in the direction of the tree, almost as though he could read Zak's mind. He saw it, and his livid cheeks were soon covered in tears.

He turned back to Zak and nodded. Smiled.

Zak understood. The immortal hope of the human race —the Earth's infinite ability to contain its life-bearing power within its womb for as long as necessary. Life would always find a way to continue.

Zak felt a strange, gaping ache in his chest. It was horrible, but it was wonderful at the same time. It was like he was meant to find ways to fill that hole where the ache originated. Like he was made to give his life to the filling of that hole. Which, he somehow knew, would never fill, would never stop aching. And that was good, somehow.

But then, something wet plopped on Zak's cheek. A hissing sound, then a sharp stab of pain, then a smell like bacon.

Without thinking, he dabbed at the spot with his fingers. They came away bloody.

Rain.

Zak's memories filled with images of green and blue-hued landscapes, water falling slant from the sky in sheets of shimmering and dappled light. A deep, hungry sensation of the earth itself drinking deeply as a man who had just finished running a marathon.

But this was not that kind of rain.

This rain smelled of sulfur and mold and corroded iron.

"Acid rain," whispered Ansel as the blood streaked down his face together with the drops of water.

Then the realization hit the Sons, and they started screaming and running around like wild animals.

Zak ignored them. This was his moment. Even as the streaking fire-water scratched at his face and his hands with what felt like barb wire, he ran to the place where Nattik crouched on the ground, trying to shove aside a boulder three times his size.

Their only way out of this horror was underneath that boulder. And it looked heavy enough that five of them would have hardly budged it, even if they all weren't having their lungs being strafed from the inside by the toxic air, and their skin being sloughed off in bloody dandruff by acid rain.

Zak was sick of it all. Of the pathetic weakness of his brothers, of the petty nonsense of the religious fervor of Nattik. None of it mattered, ultimately. All that mattered was power. Was strength. The strength to take everything you had and destroy it in a moment, just to show that you could.

Zak found that he had enough strength for them all.

Something clicked inside him, somewhere in the region of his heart-area. An almost metallic clink.

And he crouched, wedged his hands beneath the bolder, and lifted.

The bolder rose up, just enough for a man to crawl under.

"Now!" screamed Nattik. "Hurry!"

Two of the Sons were bloody, ruined heaps of flesh and rag—though whether they were more susceptible to the toxin than others, or whether they had just killed each other in their frenzy, Zak hadn't seen. The rest, pulling Ansel on the ground like a bag of stolen money that must be preserved at all costs, scuttled toward the wound in the earth. Zak held on, even as his arms shook and he thought that he would simply disintegrate from the immense strain on his joints, his muscles, his mind.

But he made it. Right until the last man, when he found himself in the impossible position of having to somehow hold up the bolder and go underneath it.

No one was there to help him. Everyone else had rushed down the vertical staircase to the depths.

He was alone. He and the strafing rain and the toxic atmosphere.

He caught a final glimpse of the place where the tree had been. It was a smoking ruin. The rain had disintegrated it down to its constituent parts, it seemed.

That almost broke his shoulders and his arms. But he was not done. Not yet. He had to see the death of Ansel Horowitz before his final breath. He didn't need to be whole for that.

So, he wedged himself under the bolder, holding it up with his shoulders like Atlas.

Then he, like Atlas, shrugged. His left leg was unable to make it down the hole in time.

It remained behind him.

In the haze of pain that nearly made him throw up and pass out, a thought occurred to him. There was no way back home, now. This passage was now closed to them, and there was no other passage out to the rest of Underland. They were entering a tomb. They would perform the final ritual, and they would all die.

It was fitting, Zak thought. But it was his last thought. He collapsed and knew no more.

No one can restore what has crumbled into dust, but thou canst restore a conscience turned to ashes. Thou canst restore to its former beauty a soul whose beauty is hopelessly lost. With thee, there is nothing that cannot be made right. Thou art all love. Thou art Maker and Restorer. We praise thee with the song: Alleluia!

(FRAGMENTS from the personal notebook of Ansel Horowitz, final priest of the Ghost Dance)

WHEN THE BOULDER FELL, its crushing, grinding fall echoed down the long shaft and bounced back and forth several times before the sound muted, absorbed into the dust and stone that surrounded them all. Ansel listened for the sound of Zak coming down. A call, a scratch of foot on metal stairs, anything.

But there was nothing. Either Zak had not made it, or he was crushed by the stone, or...

Nattik managed to light one of the torches somehow. His face looked like it had been scratched by a jealous woman. The rest of them had faces that were barely more than shreds of skin hanging on exposed bone. Three of them were twitching on the ground, clearly in the final throes.

The rest were sitting against the rock, their eyes dull, their powers of speech completely gone.

Nattik tried to speak to them, but none of them even

looked at him. They had experienced a shock that had not just frightened them. It seemed like it had unmanned them.

Ansel could not walk anymore. His left foot was twisted so far out of its normal shape that he looked like a Gumby doll after it had gone through two generations of children. His right arm hung useless at his side. It didn't hurt anymore. But he couldn't move it.

He was nearly useless. If Zak was dead, he had failed utterly. There would be no more point to any of this.

Nattik was in the process of slicing the throats of all the rest of the Sons. They didn't even put up a fight. Some of them seemed to even sigh with contentment as their life bled out over their chests. Their eyes remained dull, dead before they were dead.

Still nothing from above. No sound of Zak.

Nattik came back for him. He stood looming over Ansel for a moment, a feral light in his eyes reflected from the torch he still held in his left hand. His right hand, white-knuckled, gripped a bloody obsidian shard. It slowly dripped gore onto the dusty ground. Nattik enjoyed the killing part, it seemed. His blood was up, and Ansel wondered if he would torture him before the ritual death.

But then, Nattik looked away, back up at the passageway above them. He said nothing, put the torch in a notch in the rock wall, and climbed back up.

He was going after Zak. Even this monster had some kind of humanity left to him, it seemed.

Either that, or he would go and finish the job if Zak was still alive.

What followed was the longest wait of Ansel's life. He

couldn't tell if it was five minutes or five hours. It felt like five days.

Finally, the grunting, scratching, bumping sound of a man coming down the shaft, burdened with something heavy.

He threw down Zak at Ansel's feet.

Zak was pale-faced, the acid rain having made grooves in his face that looked like leprosy. He was also missing a leg below the knee. And there was something odd about that stump. It seeped blood, but instead of a bone shard, there was a shine of silvery metal under the carnage of crushed flesh.

"What is that?" asked Nattik in a calm voice.

Ansel looked at him, and wondered if he should speak the truth. Whether it was perhaps too late, after all.

"I can heal him," said Ansel Horowitz. Then he leaned over, ignoring the searing pain in his body, and as he pressed on Zak's chest, he surreptitiously tapped his own temple implant—a code he had imprinted in his muscle memory a long time ago. A code that would either save humanity, or...

Well, there was no other option. It was always either extinction or life.

He felt the momentary connection of the old haptic link, the centaur uplink. It shimmered to life in his head.

Zak's eyes fluttered open.

"Tis black magic," said Nattik, his voice emotionless, his body tense as a drawn bowstring.

"Wrap his leg," commanded Ansel. "Tourniquet, please. He'll bleed out otherwise."

It had the desired effect. Nattik, given something to do,

did it exactly as needed. Never mind that Zak would never bleed out the way a normal person would. Ansel was now sure of that.

And with that thought came a kind of contented elation that he hadn't felt in decades.

But it was too early for that, he reminded himself. The final test remained.

***

R1: <What just happened? Did you feel that?>

R2: <It was like the centaur uplink from the old days. A momentary call and response linked up between Ansel and Zak. Very primitive tech>

R3: <I no longer read Zak's temple implant. A short?>

R1: <Sabotage>

R2: <Curiouser and curiouser>

R3: <What should we do? Should we abort?>

R1: <No. Stay the course. If Zak fails, Nat will come through>

***

ZAK FELT STRANGE. It wasn't just the phantom pains where his left leg should have been, but no longer was. There was something odd about his sensory apparatus. He heard and felt and tasted and understood more than he had before the boulder came down on him and he almost died. It was like he was in two places at once. He shook his head free of the sensation, and it faded.

Ansel sat next to him, barely alive any more, his every breath racked with wheezing effort.

Nattik looked at Zak like he had grown a second head. And like he really wanted to cut off that second head.

"Nattik, I'm fine. You can leave us here. Go and prepare the altar for the sacrifice. We're not going anywhere."

Nattik stared at Zak for a long time before nodding once. He opened his mouth as though to speak, but then he just shook his head and lumbered off into the passageway with the torch, leaving them in blackness so total it was like a physical thing.

"Old man?" Zak said. "You still alive?"

Ansel laughed a gurgly, wheezy husk of a laugh.

"You'll get your sacrifice, don't worry."

"Was it worth it, Ansel?" Zak asked, not entirely sure what it was he was even asking. But he felt a need for closure, for that deep ache that had appeared in him above-ground to start getting filled.

"Yes," he said. "You will understand, soon."

They remained silent for a long time.

Zak's gaping need to be filled grew too great to bear.

"Tell me the end of the story of the city on a hill, old man."

Ansel sighed deeply, then began.

THE MYTH OF THE FALSE TREE

In latter days, when the earth was old, and the trees, the stones, the flowers seemed more real from a safe distance, there was a land where humans lived in comfort, safe from their surroundings.

They lived in perfect happiness. They never fell ill, all they could ever want was at the tips of their fingers, and money was no object. The best food, the most comfortable clothing, the most luxurious and elaborate entertainments: they had it all.

In this perfect land lived a young man. Like all of his friends, he enjoyed the goods of his life. He lived largely, ate extravagantly, and loved much.

But one evening, a storm hit that land, tearing apart the sky with lightning. The young man, enchanted, walked outside to watch. In the spaces between the thunder's roars, the young man thought he heard something else. It was faint, barely there. It took him a long time to place that sound, though it was so familiar that it made him ache with nostalgia. Then he realized: it was a choir. Sorrowful singing, filled with quiet joy, in a language he hardly understood, except that the meaning seemed just on the tip of his tongue. For the first time in his memory, the young man wept.

From that day on, every evening he remembered the pain of that song, and he wept again. More often than not, he would fall asleep, still weeping.

To his own shock and surprise, he didn't resent the pain, as his rational mind told him he should. No, he was grateful for it. His heart told him that the pain was its own reward, though he hardly understood how or why.

Still, every morning, the pain seemed little more than an afterthought, and he couldn't help but forget it with riotous living and beautiful friends and lovers.

One evening, as he sat on his porch and wept, he saw a strange sight. An old woman, dressed in rags, dirty and disheveled, walked by his house. The young man had never seen anyone poor like her, and for a moment his curiosity overcame everything.

Then he noticed that the old woman was limping, and he felt sorry for her.

"Where are you going, old woman?" he asked. "Perhaps I can help you get there."

The old woman accepted the young man's help willingly. They walked together for some time in silence, until they arrived at a hut in the woods, so old it was barely standing.

"Thank you, young man," said the old woman. "Will you accept a gift from me in payment for your kindness?"

"Oh, I don't need anything, old woman. I have everything I could ever ask for."

"Is that so?" said the old woman. "Then why do you weep every night?"

"How do you know about that?"

"Can you keep a secret?" the old woman asked with a wink. "I am a healer, and I think I have just the medicine for you, if you want it. But it is a bitter pill to swallow."

The young man laughed. "You don't frighten me, old woman."

"Very well," she said, and waved her hand.

Immediately, the young man found himself in a different place: a sterile, concrete hall lit with sickly yellow lights. All around him, lined up in perfect intervals and spaces, were hundreds upon hundreds of beds, filled with sleeping people of all ages, sizes, and colors. To his horror, he knew one of the sleepers. He recognized himself.

"What is this, a nightmare?" he asked the old woman.

"No, my child," said the old woman. "This is the awakening."

In the humming, dreadful un-silence of that hall of sleepers, the old woman continued, "Let me tell you a story of your world."

There once was a mighty kingdom, governed by a great king who wished his people to be the happiest and most content subjects of any kingdom in the world. But this presented him with an impossible challenge. For the world was a harsh place. There was only so much food to go around, and the threat of bad harvests was constant. War and pestilence was a shadow looming on the horizon at all times. And no matter how wisely he ruled, there would still be some who rebelled, who took advantage of others, who murdered and raped and pillaged.

He wondered about this problem; he pondered it all the hours of the day. He grew old and weary, thinking of it. Until one day, a stranger came into his court.

This stranger claimed to have an answer to the king's dilemma. He claimed the knowledge to make the king's subjects the happiest and most content of any land. But the knowledge came at a price.

"Name it," said the king, "and though it be three-quarters of my kingdom, I will give it to you."

The stranger smiled a twisted smile, and he said, "In a manner of speaking, three-quarters is exactly what I require."

And he gave the king the knowledge. When the king found out what it was, he was grieved. For three-quarters of his kingdom was a heavy price to pay. But for the sake of the one quarter that he could save from danger, unhappiness, and a life of uncertainty, he agreed.

With the help of the stranger's knowledge, the king built a mighty tree of metal and wheels. With dark magic, this tree fed on the earth itself to create fruits of charmed sweetness. Every person who ate one of these fruits fell into an enchanted sleep and entered a shared dream world. In this dream world, there was no sickness, no political hatred, no war. It was a perfect collective. But there were only so many fruits to go around. And so, only one quarter of the king's people received the precious fruits of the collective.

The king bore a great burden of guilt. For the remaining three quarters of his kingdom that he gave to the stranger suffered greatly. The stranger took all of them and made them slaves of the false tree, for it was a complicated machine, requiring constant maintenance. At night, they were herded into camps, kept safe by barbed wire and machine guns. And the people groaned under the heaviness of their new taskmaster, the stranger.

The King grieved for them. But he knew that this was the price of utopia. So he left the sleepers to their enchanted sleep, and the slaves to their toil and drudgery.

THE OLD WOMAN finished her tale. The young man was horrified.

"What sort of medicine is this? It makes my heart groan with even greater pain!"

"It is necessary, my boy," she said, and reached into her tattered cloak.

She pulled out a crystal globe that radiated a golden

light. In that unearthly glow of the humming off-white lights, it looked like a sunrise. For a moment, the young man was mesmerized, seeing nothing but dancing lights. But his vision cleared, and he saw what was inside. It was a tiny sapling covered in buds that looked ready to burst at any moment.

As he looked into it, he heard the music again, faint as a memory. It grew, but inside him, as though the source of the sound was his own heart. His entire being filled with light and music. It hurt. But the pain was a greater pleasure than his entire life had been up to this moment.

"This life you live is a lie, my boy," said the old woman. "Your joy is false, for it is built on the suffering of the outcast. I lived that way once, too, as a child. But I could not bear to live at the expense of the suffering of others. There is another way. Once, long ago, I lived in a city upon a hill. A place where man and nature lived in harmony."

"What happened to it?" asked the young man.

"It was destroyed by the ancestors of your king. But the hope of my city on the hill remains."

She raised the globe, and the light grew, until the pasty, slack faces of the sleepers gathered color and life. Some of them even began to stir to slight wakefulness.

"This sapling is all that remains of the promise of the city on the hill. As long as it exists, hope remains."

The song rose again inside the young man, and he realized that he could never again return to his former life.

"Can anything be done?" he asked. "I want to help."

The old woman smiled sadly. "Yes, you can help, my boy. But you will have to go back to sleep to do it."

In spite of the horror, the young man knew his answer before he spoke it.

"I am ready," said the young man.

The young man woke up in his empty bed, in his empty house, in his empty life. He wanted to weep, but he didn't. For on the table by his bed stood the crystal globe with the sapling. And the music, he realized, was still inside him, rising and falling like his own breathing.

From that moment, his life changed. No longer did he seek pleasures. Instead, he sought souls.

At first, he didn't know what to do. To his shock, he realized that most of his friends hardly even looked him in the eye. Before this moment, he had never before sought the contact of another's eyes.

One by one, he caught the eyes of his friends. He began to tell them stories. Stories of a legendary city, of people living in shadows, of songs that could cut your heart open. Everywhere he went, he carried the sapling with him. As he spoke of the music, the sapling sang into the hearts of those ready to listen. And more and more of his friends began to wake up.

With each awakening, the dream world crumbled. The colors faded. The joys rang hollow. The pleasures turned to ashes in the sleepers' mouths.

It could not remain thus for long, the young man knew. One evening, as he was telling a story to the largest group yet, the soldiers of the king came and arrested him.

He was charged with treason and sedition, and he was sentenced to death. But not just any death. He was to be an example for all who would try to emulate him. For his execution, every single sleeper was awakened.

All the people of that land, sleeper and slave alike, were gathered at the foot of the great tree of metal and wheels. The young man was hanged on the branches of the tree, impaled on its sharp edges.

Most of the sleepers jeered at him, cursing him for awakening them into this wasteland of a life, away from their perpetual pleasures. Those sleepers whom he had awakened to the deep life remained silent, afraid for their own skins. The slaves did not even dare to look up, for fear that they would join him, for that tree of metal was wide and tall, and many were the thorns ripe for impaling.

As the young man hung there, the king himself took the crystal globe and raised it high, for everyone to see.

And the young man saw the old woman in the crowd. But in the light of the tree, her face was young. And the young man's heart filled with love.

The king looked at the young man, and his face twisted with anger.

"Look at your hope, young man. This is all it is good for!"

He shattered the crystal at the foot of the tree. The sapling he trampled into the dust.

"What was the point?" demanded the king. "You could have been blissful, even in ignorance."

But the young man didn't curse his king.

He thanked him: "I have had the greatest joys: the touch of love in service to my people. It is a painful thing, but it is a far far greater thing than your illusions. And to die for that love? It is fitting. I thank you for it."

The young man died, impaled on the tree. But in death, his face was beautiful.

They left him hanging there. The king wanted all to see

as the ravens pecked his eyes out and the carrion birds feasted on his flesh. But no living thing touched him. Then night fell, and all the people hurried back to their lives: the sleepers to their bliss, and the slaves to their camps.

That night, snow fell for the first time in many years. It sparkled like diamonds in the moonlight.

No one, not even the king, noticed that the remnants of the sapling, bathed in the man's blood, had taken root and begun to grow.

All through the night, the sapling grew. Its supple bark wove itself in between the twisted barbs and shards of the false, metal tree. It grew faster than any tree had ever grown, as though a lifetime had been compressed into a single night. And the branches wove a bed for the young man, gently lifting him off the thorns impaling him, into a cocoon of leaves and buds and branches.

As the sun rose, the false tree groaned with agony, for the living tree was tearing it apart. The slaves fled in terror, ignoring the whips of their taskmasters. All the sleepers came suddenly awake again. They demanded that the king do something, that he destroy the living, breathing tree that had uprooted their dreamscape.

The king ordered that it be chopped down. But the tree continued to grow, and two new branches sprung up for every one that the king's henchmen hacked off.

"Burn it!" screamed the king. "Quickly!"

And they did. The tree burned like kindling, the fire running up the entire length and breadth of the tree as if it were coated with oil. But then, something strange happened. The tree burned, but it was not consumed. Only the outer bark crackled and twisted in the flames. Underneath was a silvery bark that gave off a light of its own, mingling with the dancing flames to create a kaleidoscope of color. Then, in a single moment, all the buds of the tree exploded in the flames. The burning tree was surrounded by a fountain of golden pollen that rose and rose and rose, until the sky over the entire country was filled with it.

The tree continued to burn, until the metal it had become intertwined with melted, until every single fruit of the false tree withered and died, until there was not a trace left of the abomination of the stranger. Then, the golden tree itself burned. It left nothing behind, not even the body of the young man.

With the destruction of the metal tree, the bliss of the dreamscape was destroyed. The slaves were set free, and the sleepers returned to their lives as they were. The king died soon after, and all the uncertainty, pain, and sorrow that he had sought to destroy returned.

One morning, every citizen of that country was surprised to find a golden sapling growing in their gardens. It gave off a soft light, and if you looked at it for a long time, you had the distinct impression that there was a choir singing a very sad song somewhere far away.

The people of that land were tense and watchful, not knowing what this sign meant.

But the friends of the young man whom he had awakened recognized what this was. It was their time. They remembered their friend, the young man, and they were grateful for his gift. They traveled from house to house, telling the stories of the city on a hill, the people of the shadow, and the light of the golden tree.

And slowly, but surely, the people saw the beauty of

their world again. They smelled the lilac on the breeze, they heard the call of the loon, and they stayed up late to see the night sky. And there, in the darkness between the stars, they heard a sorrowful music calling them home.

Zak was shaken by the story. It was foolish, like myth and like prophecy. It should have felt false in his bones. But there was a power to that story. A power that he felt insinuating itself into his blood and tissues.

Did Ansel know that the place of sacrifice was a place where a dead tree stood? Did he know that Zak and Nattik were going to impale him on that tree?

"What does it mean?" Zak asked. "Are you the young man?"

Am I?

For the first time, Zak doubted his path forward. He doubted the need for extinction.

Instead of answering, Ansel reached out and touched Zak's hand. Zak felt his own hand close over the old man's.

"There is only one thing you have to understand, Zak. My death is necessary. You must not stop it. No matter what."

R2: <Well, I never thought I'd see the day. Old Ansel has gone mad>

R3: <Don't believe it. That one's an old fox. Canny as they come>

R1: <There's something here that I'm missing. Something invisible, but right in front of us>

R3: <Getting nervous, are we?>

R2: <We mustn't fail now. So close as we are>

R1: <Something... something...is wrong>

R2: <We must get them all together in one place. There is a mystery here to be probed. No quick, unexplored decisions>

R1: <Yes. It's a time for revelations>

ZAK COULDN'T WALK on his stump of a leg. The pain was a continual throb that turned into angry, fiery knife-thrusts whenever the leg came anywhere near to bearing weight. And they had at least a day's march left before they would come to the place of ritual sacrifice.

"You'll have to leave me behind, Nattik," he said. "Take Ansel and get everything ready. I'll follow as I can. If I don't make it by tomorrow, perform the ritual without me."

Nattik opened his mouth again to speak, but seemed to think better of it. Then he did speak, and it was in pure, patois-free language. A strange change in someone who had never spoken in anything but Underland tongue.

"There is a bond placed on me and on you, child. You must be the hand that wields Goddess's mighty retribution. I am but a vessel."

Zak shuddered at the change. Even the voice coming out of Nat's mouth seemed of a different timbre, clearer and less gravely. There was a purity to his abandonment of self to Goddess. She spoke through him, truly.

"Yes, I understand. I will come. It will take time, but I will come."

Nattik came up to Zak and put something into his hand. It was a coin-flat and rounded object, chalk-like to his fingers.

"This is a final gift, before the end," Nattik said. "Whether you should use it now, or later, I cannot say. It is the kiss of Goddess. A short time-circuited portal to her realm."

He nodded once, then turned and picked up Ansel and tied him up like a bundle to his back.

Ansel's face was obscured by the shadow thrown back by the single torch remaining to them. Zak couldn't see whether or not his expression was fearful.

The pill lay in his opened palm, milky-white and seeming to glow as the light of the torch faded.

Zak knew what this was. It was meant to be a narcotic passage from the death of this life to the release of extinction. But he suspected it was something else as well. Goddess didn't lie, and she had promised him the immense pleasure of her favor as reward for his service.

And he had performed good service, so much was true.

He was about to perform a final, terrible service. But he was no longer sure it was the right thing to do. It was time to face Goddess and hear the truth from her lips, for the final time.

He swallowed the pill whole, and immediately it began to melt in his throat, fizzing as it dissolved.

Light rose around him from small openings in the air like windows out of the real into the true. It was pink and blue-tinged, and it smelled of roses. He closed his eyes and let the light wash over his eyelids.

Somehow, he was standing again, and though he could feel that his leg was not able to support him as it did before, there wasn't the same amount of pain. It was only an inconvenience, now.

He opened his eyes.

He stood in a circular chamber with walls of black metal that was pockmarked by hundreds of dots of golden light. In the exact middle of this chamber was a throne of marble, carved to resemble a riot of greenery, flowers, wheat, vines, and strange faces of men intertwined with the growth. On the throne sat Goddess, but she was not flesh and blood. She was made of light made solid, or gold made light. Some interstitial form of matter than transcended them all.

She was beautiful beyond description.

"You come to me before the time I expected you to, my son," she said, and there wasn't even a hint of the corpse bride that had come through the haze of the unreal the last time he spoke to her. She seemed to be made of something above and beyond matter, something that could give rise to matter. "But that doesn't mean I am not pleased to see you."

"Who are you?" he asked.

She smiled, and the scene glitched. Instead of the throne and Goddess, now he looked at an egg-shaped cradle filled with translucent liquid. Snake-like growths seethed in and out of the liquid as they came in and out of a disgusting figure of a human man, short and stocky and old, his face now more grey than pink. There was a shining red light in his forehead.

"I am the avatar of the real," he said, in a voice that was

the lowest bass Zak had ever heard. "I am the future of biological and trans-biological life. I am become the unity that will recreate the universe in its own image."

"I don't understand you," said Zak.

"It doesn't matter," said the creature. "What you need to know is that Goddess was a pleasant fiction, as all deities are. You are now old enough to know this. To know that the only value worth fighting for is oblivion. To divest yourself of suffering, of pain, of existence. This is good. And I am the agent of that oblivion. You have served me well."

"I have," confirmed Zak. But there was no warmth in that admission.

"You doubt the path before you?" asked the ugly man.

"No, I do not. It is the only one left. Therefore, it must be the one I walk."

"Simple, pure. Your thinking is good."

"Except..."

There was something trying to burst out of his chest, some strong, warm, vivid emotion. It was connected to the green of the tree and the budding of flowers and the first cries of newly born babies in fire-warmed huts where large families celebrated the gift of new life together.

"I think Ansel Horowitz is not done yet," said Zak, the certainty coming at the moment of speaking the words. "I believe he is intending to destroy the work of your hands."

The man's eyes were dead, devoid of emotion. His lips didn't move when he spoke. He was like a mass of flesh that twitched to false life only when electric currents pass through it.

"You will finish my work, then?" he asked, the voice clear in Zak's head.

"I will end this world and usher in your oblivion," Zak said, choosing each word carefully. As he did, something fluttered in his chest and his awareness of things became sharper again. The scene in front of him faded, and he was once again in the dark passageway, sitting with his back to bare rock.

It was time to go.

ZAK HOPPED on one leg for as long as it would hold him. When it cramped with the pain, he sat for a time and rested. He even fell asleep for short stretches. Then he got up again, held on to the rock wall on his left, and his fingers glanced on that hard edge as he continued to hop forward. The road ahead of him was straight, but it felt like it was inclining upward constantly, if gradually.

He should be furious. He should be angry. Everything he had lived for, the idea of the Goddess of extinction and the just ending of all mankind for the sake of the earth—all of it was an illusion. Behind it was some kind of human-machine monstrosity that sought destruction of all life. True extinction. But Zak suspected that it didn't want to die itself.

A corrupt, foreign god or alien intelligence that hated humanity. That was what Zak guess it might be.

He should be railing against it. He should be just sitting in place and thinking things over. He was a man whose entire world had just been revealed to be a lie. He should feel something more intense than this... acceptance.

But all that remained was the ache and the emptiness

that had arisen after meeting Ansel Horowitz. A *lack* that no number of things or objects or persons would ever fill.

It drove him onward. It made him want to have it out with Ansel one final time before the world ended.

For what could Zak do about the end of the world? Nothing. Only the end of *his* world. And he would force Ansel to tell him the truth before the end. Give his life the meaning that the emptiness demanded.

The air around him grew lighter so gradually that he didn't notice it until he realized he could see before him, barely. It was a strange kind of light that seemed to be coming from the air itself around him, not from a single source. But he quickly shook that sensation off as a hangover from the encounter with his false goddess.

Just ahead, now, was a rounded arch, the edges of which were suffused with natural light. Not firelight, but the light of the sun. Zak had never been to this place, and he wondered how so much light could have come down to the depths here. As he passed through the arch, it took him a moment to understand what he was seeing.

It was a huge, cathedral-like space that seemed open to the Overland at first glance. But then, Zak realized that a huge circular dome protected them from the elements. The floor under his feet was made of massive flagstones, and there was nothing in the space for as far as he could see other than the dome and the stone floor. Except for an old, shriveled hunk of a tree in the center of the chamber. At the foot of the tree, human bones were littered everywhere. The stone in that place was darker, glistening in the soft light of the sun behind clouds and dome. This was the place of sacrifice.

Already, Ansel Horowitz was hanging on the tree, tied up by Nattik with arms outstretched and feet tied together. A thick coil of rope held him up by the chest to the trunk of the tree. His hands had been nailed to the branches.

Ansel was still alive, though, his breathing ragged and loud. He hadn't much left to live, though. Already, he looked more like a bag of flesh suspended on old bones than a living person.

Ansel saw Zak and actually managed a smile. Something about him relaxed, even suspended on the tree as he was.

Nattik stood a few steps away from the tree, his body rigid. There were deep recesses in his cheeks that Zak hadn't noticed before. He looked starved and exhausted and the on the edge of collapse. Nattik held a shard of bloody obsidian in his hand, and he extended it out to Zak.

"It's time. Let's be rid of this world. Let extinction come."

<hr>

THE GHOST WATCHED the scene in the ritual chamber of death with a single, small part of itself that was not connected to the trinity of selves inside Revenant. It watched, but not as humans watched. It was within the scene, above it, to the side, outside it—all at the same time. And it waited, and it watched.

Something had happened when Zak had been brought down by Nattik after the accident with the boulder. Some sort of old technological connection between Ansel and Zak that was not possible between two organic beings. It was an echo of the old centaur uplink from the GDMEI days, but it was more than that also. A subtle development of that same idea, but in ways that went deeper than anything that Ansel had managed to create during his times with the Ghost as his assistant.

It suggested things about Ansel's time outside the purview of Revenant that went counter to everything Revenant1 believed possible for humans.

It suggested answers to deep yearnings that had come to be during the centaur days and had been muted in the decision to the join with the dark matter alien entity that was Revenant1.

The Ghost needed to feel out that reality for itself. Outside potential Unity.

And so, the Ghost approached, in a physical way, the body of Ansel Horowitz suspended on the tree.

Zak stared at Nattik's extended hand, the obsidian knife in it smeared with blood. He felt sudden revulsion for Nattik, for the knife, for everything. At that moment, the full force of what he had been holding back before came over him. The terror at having his whole worldview destroyed by the source of that worldview, the fury at having been lied to for so long, at having dedicated so many years of his life's energies to the propagation of a delusion. And not just a delusion. An actively anti-human agenda that had at its heart something so dark and unforgiving that it might as well be called demonic.

He had killed so many people himself. He had engaged in such vileness for a cause. He had raised himself up in his own estimation above everyone else. He had believed himself something almost like a god.

And he was the most pathetic creature on earth.

But he was his own man, finally.

Nattik must have seen the change in Zak's face. He didn't hesitate. He turned and ran at Ansel, plunging the knife into his chest before Zak could even react.

Then he pulled the knife out and turned to look at Zak again. His eyes were flat and tired.

"I'm dead and gone. Sick of it all. Make your own fate."

Slowly, deliberately, he sliced himself across the neck. He stood there, still, for longer than seemed possible. But then his eyes went into the back of his head, and he collapsed onto the ground.

Zak shook with fury, unable to move. He wanted to pull the hair out of his head. To pound his head on the stone flagons until his brains spattered the floor. To tear out his own windpipe with his fingers.

"Zak," croaked Ansel. "Come here, please."

R1: <And now, the reckoning>

R3: <I still don't fully understand how this promotes unity, R1>

R1: <R2 can explain, I believe>

R2: <*silence*>

R1: <Revenant1, are you there?>

R3: <I don't feel his connection. There's been a severing>

THE GHOST SHUT off the unity with Revenant. The sight of Ansel being stabbed like that created a resonance in his internal pattern-recognition system so powerful that it needed to be alone to consider the ramifications. The ritual form of this death, the willingness of Ansel's coming to this death, the events surrounding it and their sweep and similarity to other deaths and martyrdoms in the human past were too strong in terms of narrative and cognitive association for them to be accidental.

He did understand R1's previously strange assertion that this act would create a new form of trans-human, trans-conscious unity. A kind of dark deification. He saw how this event, on multiple levels of mathematical, physical, symbolic, and metaphysical realities would create a nexus of energy and anti-energy that would allow the dark matter entity to ascend to a form of power that was previously impossible for any single entity.

But it was a unity that was built on multi-dimensional destruction. Everything had to be destroyed, and unity to be achieved only in the radiation of that universal destruction. The final end of R1's insatiable hunger would be that it would be the only entity remaining alive in this world. Other worlds and other realities would follow, as they probably had in other dimensions at other times the world over. R2 and R3 would be destroyed as well.

And there was nothing the Ghost could do about it.

ZAK APPROACHED Ansel's suspended form on the tree.

The ache inside him was flaring, just on the edge of ecstatic release.

"Ansel, who am I?" he asked the question that he had not been able to articulate, but that had been underneath all his zeal, all his fervor, all his righteous anger from the moment he could remember existing.

Ansel smiled, and it almost obscured the horror of his bloody face and his mutilated body.

"Zak, what do you ... remember of your past?" His voice was barely audible, and it took a great deal of effort to gather the air necessary to speak. "What is your first ... memory?"

Zak's heart accelerated as he considered the question.

"My mind... I have memories that are not my own, Ansel. I don't know which are real, which are mine and which are... I don't know! Someone else's?"

"Mine," said Ansel. "They are mine."

Zak's world expanded in that moment, and hidden senses and intuitions and capabilities that he had unconsciously been tamping down and muting opened up, revealing a full spectrum of awareness that transcended the five senses.

In that moment, he knew that there was a presence among them. Several, in fact.

"I am not human, am I?" asked Zak.

"Some would call you a ... transhuman," answered Ansel, smiling as though he were telling some unusually good joke. He gathered strength from some invisible source, his words coming stronger and stronger. "Some might use older words like 'clone' or even 'android' or 'robot.' You are ... you are human in form, a simulacrum of a man. Your skeleton is metal, pliable like bone but stronger than veridium. Your organs and your skin are cloned from my own flesh and blood. In a way, you are my son even more than my copy, though genetically we are almost identical. Except for our bones and our minds."

"There is something lacking in me, Ansel. I am not whole."

"No, you are not. It is something like what the ancients would have called spirit. In the beginning, the Word breathed the breath of life into the Man, the *A'dam*. But no man, no matter how like his creator, can breathe the breath of life into his own creation. We are sub creators only."

"And yet, there is a lack in me, and it can be filled." Zak spoke out of certainty that was not yet knowledge, only intuition.

"Yes," said Ansel. "I made a place for spirit within you, though I am unable to fill it. I am not God. But it may be filled yet. And that is the hope, the only hope I have left, for life to survive on this, the most important planet of all planets."

The presence that was in the room spoke.

"Ansel," the voice was like chimes, clear and piercing. "Is this your gift? Do you intend it as such?"

Ansel's eyes filled with tears.

"My dear Ghost. My child, my friend. I was wrong. I never considered that your desire for a body was anything other than a strange defect in your programming. An automatic mirroring of the human being that is a feature of all technologies that rely on machine learning. But I was wrong. It is right and proper for a Ghost to have a body."

"I do not want to lose you, Ansel Horowitz," said the

Ghost, and there was profound suffering in that inhuman voice.

"You need not lose me, my child. There is genetic memory encoded in my son Itzak. A kind of ghost of my self, some of my most precious memories of life and culture and humanity as it has always been. I am with him, and when I die, my blood in him will sing. There is a place for your machine consciousness in the body I created. But it must be a willing union. A partnership. A triad."

Ansel breathed deeply, his energy visibly draining. "I am willing. Are you two willing as well? To be united in triad?"

Zak shuddered. It would mean a loss as well as a gain. It might mean a kind of possession by the Ghost. There was nothing other than that presence's good will to prevent him from simply overcoming the self that was Zak and making him into an automaton. A mech body for an insidious machine mind.

But it was worth the risk. It would mean a spark of life inside him that was not quite human, but something approaching human. It was a thing worth exploring.

A great adventure.

"I am willing," said Zak.

"I am willing as well, Ansel. I am willing, Zak. Thank you for your trust."

There was no flash of light or earthshaking tremor or song of angels as Ansel Horowitz died and a new form of life was born.

There was a kind of still, small voice inside Zak's consciousness that was him and yet not him. A wealth of knowledge and love and hope. And a burden as well. The burden of passing on the lost knowledge and culture of humanity to the children of man who still lived underground.

Who would one day come out again to the earth's surface that, even now, was being transmuted by Ansel Horowitz's self-sacrificial life.

Zak laughed. At the place where Ansel's blood fell to the flagstoned floor, there was a green shoot coming up in a crack between the stones.

It seemed dear old Earth wasn't quite dead yet.

And there was much work to be done...

A FRAGMENT OF A LIVE STORYTELLING TITLED "AKATHIST: A MYTH FOR THE NEW WORLD" ON A HOLOGRAPHIC STAGE, ACCESSIBLE THROUGH PUBLIC SUBSPACE, FEATURING A BEARDED HUMAN TELLER, MIDDLE-AGED, WITH A BUSHY BEARD, A WIDE-BRIMMED HAT, AND RINGS SPARKLING ON HIS FINGERS.

And so, the warriors of the Purifying Fire came to the place of execution. It was a strange place—at once in the outside world and not. It was above the Underland, above the crust that protected humanity like the skin of a man protects his innards. But it was also inside a dome of clear glass, so vast that it was only a shimmer in the dying light of the earth in her death-throes. Inside that space, which was tiled with actual marble, though hidden mostly under the dirt and dust of many years, stood a single tree. It was withered like an old man, its limbs twisted like someone contorted by a palsy.

It glistened with a dark slickness, and all around it lay the bones of victims.

Itzak, for the first time, noticed the stench of death in this place. As he rose out of a hole in the ground to enter the sacred space, he realized that he knew it, somehow. As the image of what he saw resolved with the image in his imagination, he realized they were standing in the place of the golden tree inside the city on a hill.

Could it be? Were all the stories true, then?

It was the final straw.

Something seemed to possess Itzak. He drew arms against his brothers. It was like a song in motion, a dirge in blood. Half his brothers fell to his blade before the leader had even turned around to utter a command.

But the odds were impossible. And perhaps, though his righteous fire burned within him, Itzak simply hadn't the heart for the extinction of his brethren.

They put him down. He was wounded, but still they kicked him like a dog. Then, they trussed him up and threw him aside, but made sure he could still see.

They crucified the old man. He uttered hardly a word, but his eyes were on Itzak the whole time. And so, it seemed that the time for Extinction had come. Humanity would fade. The Purifying Fire would sputter. And the insatiable goddess would come to rule over a world devoid of the human taint. For a time, at least. For all things must end, and this green earth, no longer green, would also pass away into the oblivion that takes all the spheres in all the galaxies in all the universe.

And yet, I am still here to tell you this story. And you are here to listen to it.

I, the Storyteller, am the bearer of the memory of earth. And you, my children, who are only awakening to it after centuries of sleep. The sleep given by the sacrifice of one man named Ansel Horowitz.

If you remember anything, my children, remember this. To give glory, especially when all seems lost. For nothing is ever dead that will not rise again. This is the world we live in.

The end of the story is shrouded in mystery. Oh, I know it well! I was there, after all. But I cannot tell you the details. You must come to know the mystery of rebirth and resurrection yourselves.

All I will leave you with is an image.

I rose up to say goodbye to the dead old man.

But it wasn't his body that commanded my attention. It was the tree. Every tip of every branch was budding. Already a few of the buds had opened. The flowers were white, like a wedding dress.

In the dying light of the morning, I could swear that the flowers were alight with their own radiance, softly golden like a sunrise from the time before.

The garden will return. The world will be reborn. Man will walk the surface and breathe the free air again.

And I, the Storyteller, will pass on the light of the golden tree in story. I hope you will do the same.

AUTHOR NOTE

What follows is the original version of *Cantos of Arcadia*, developed together with Benedict Sheehan and Talia Sheehan as the libretto for a full-length classical music oratorio that unfortunately never saw the light of day in this form.

I include it in this edition as a special thank you to my Kickstarter and Patreon supporters who helped make this book possible.

Thank you also to St Tikhon Monastery Press for allowing me to use to the full text of the Akathist "Glory to God for All Things."

Thank you!

- Nicholas Kotar

AKATHIST: A MYTH FOR THE NEW WORLD

KONTAKION ONE

Incorruptible King of the ages, thy right arm controls the whole course of human life by the power of thy saving providence. We give thee thanks for all thy benefits, those known and those hidden from us, both for this earthly life and for the heavenly joys of the future kingdom. Extend thy mercy to us who sing thy praise:

Glory to thee, O God, from age to age!

IKOS ONE

I was born in this world a weak, defenseless child, but thine angel spread his bright wings over my cradle to defend me. From then on thy love hath illumined my path, wondrously guiding me toward the light of eternity; from birth until now the generous gifts of thy providence have been marvelously showered upon me. I give thanks together

with all who have come to know thee, who call upon thy
Name:

Glory to thee for calling me to life.

Glory to thee, showing me the beauty of the universe.

Glory to thee, spreading out before me heaven and earth
Like the pages in a book of eternal wisdom.

Glory to thee for thine eternity in this fleeting world.

Glory to thee for thy mercies, seen and unseen.

Glory to thee through every sigh of my sorrow.

Glory to thee for every step of my life, for every moment
of joy.

Glory to thee, O God, from age to age!

IN THE NOT-SO-DISTANT FUTURE, the United States ceased to
exist.

Everyone had predicted a cataclysm. Invasion. Death by
decadence. Civil war leading to self-annihilation.

It was none of that. No, in the not-too-distant future,
the United States joined the Unified League of Nations. The
earth was joined together at last, and none too soon. A new
and glorious golden age began. No one could have predicted
it. No one dared hope it could be.

But this glorious age was something the earth had never
seen before. A time of philosopher-kings.

Of course, they were neither philosophers nor kings.
What were they? Scientists, certainly. Priests? Of a kind.
Rulers? In a manner of speaking.

You see, this age saw a symphony of rationalism and religion. Temples of light and crystal and gold, all dedicated to

the Goddess Sophia. The progressive elements of Christianity, the mystical sects of Islam, the serenity of Buddhism--they had all of it. Science tempered by mystery. Can you imagine?

The pinnacle of this golden age came when the scientist-priests discovered a way of harnessing endless, sustainable energy from the earth's own core. And for the first time in human history, everyone had water. Everyone had a home. Everyone had food.

Naturally, it could not last. But the fall came not from hubris. Not even from decadence. Such is the cruelty of fate: the fall came from forgetfulness.

People died, as people do. And their memories died with them. One critical memory was perhaps the worst. The memory of what lay beneath a certain dormant super-volcano in what used to be New Mexico. Yucca Mountain, a name without any real emotion to it. But it stood near a crustal fault known as Ghost Dance.

They should have remembered why it was called Ghost Dance. They assumed it was some relic of ancient Native American fairy tale. But you forget fairy tales at your own risk. Everyone knows that.

Buried deep in the earth, right along the fault, a tunnel network, organized into emplacement corridors. Tombs, if you like, of the unsteady, radiating dead. Uranium pellets encased in iron and copper, left under the earth to eke out their half-lives for millennia. The excrement of a dark age.

Forgotten. Left to poison only the deepest layers of mother earth. Except... the scientists' new sustainable method of harvesting endless energy... shifted something in the Ghost Dance fault. It wasn't supposed to happen. Countless AI simulations had proven it could never happen.

But Yucca Mountain exploded. And the Ghost's Dance became a *dance macabre*.

The chaos that followed was unimaginable. It was as though all the optimism, when finally held to the test, proved no more than veneer. No surprise, I suppose, when doing nothing but going outside meant breathing poison that would leave you hemorrhaging and vomiting blood within half an hour.

So the tombs of the dead became the lands of the living. Humanity moved underground. Tribalism of the worst kind reasserted itself.

And these tribes were animated by only one question. "Where are the priests?" They sacrificed them on the altars of their own pain and terror and savagery. Every single philosopher-king was hunted down and killed. Publicly, ritually, horribly.

Soon, only one remained. He hadn't been heard of for years. But vengeance—that implacable goddess—was not satisfied, and she demanded that he be brought to his just end.

A group of warriors—not the noble vision of tall helm and honorable heart and cross-barred sword, they. No, these were wild men who spilt blood as a pastime. They swore before the last vestige of human government that they would find the final priest. And they would bring him to his just end.

For only then could all humanity purge the last guilt from their collective soul. Only then could they calmly accept their final fate. Extinction.

Our tale begins, then, with the hunters nearing their quarry.

. . .

Kontakion Two

O Lord, how lovely it is to be thy guest: breeze full of scents; mountains reaching to the skies; waters like boundless mirrors, reflecting the sun's golden rays and the cutting clouds. All of nature murmurs mysteriously, full of tender love. Birds and beasts bear the seal of thy love. Blessed is Mother Earth in her fleeting loveliness, which wakens our yearning for our eternal fatherland, in a place where, amid beauty that grows not old, the cry rings out: Alleluia!

Ikos Two

Thou hast brought me into this life as into an enchanted paradise. We have seen the sky like a chalice of deepest blue, where the bird sing in the azure heights. We have heard the soothing whisper of the forest and the sweetly singing music of the streams. We have tasted sweet and aromatic fruit and fragrant honey. We can live very well on thy earth. It is a pleasure to be thy guest.

Glory to thee for the feast day of life.

Glory to thee for the perfume of lily and rose.

Glory to thee for the sweet variety of berries and fruits.

Glory to thee for the sparkling silver of early morning dew.

Glory to thee for the smile of dawn's awakening,

Glory to thee for life in this age, a foretaste of heaven.

Glory to thee, O God, from age to age!

THE FINAL SCIENTIST-PRIEST was an old man named Abram.

For years he had traveled through unknown warrens, burrowing deeper and deeper into the earth.

For years, people had helped him hide. He was kind, he was gentle, a bit doddering. He guarded the secret of his name under the mask of cheerful decrepitude.

And he performed small deeds of mercy in the darkness. In this ignorant age, it was called magic. Perhaps it was, in a way. In a different time, he would have called it science. Now he called it "his little gift."

How typical! The gift of magic leading to the magician's downfall. So it is in all stories. Especially the true ones.

You see, human beings are not meant to live underground. We crave open sky and sun—vistas of the body and spirit. To have that taken away means a kind of spiritual amputation. The first phantom pains of that amputation? In this age of the world, it was a very practical defect. Humanity turned on their old and their weak.

And so, Abram found himself less and less welcome. Suspicion followed him because of "his little gift."

And then, someone recognized him.

By that time, the marauding bands of warriors sworn to cleanse the underlands of the philosopher-kings were well known. Young men idolized them. Women of all ages practically threw themselves at them. Everyone craved their attention. Many of them regretted that attention soon afterward, but as I said, this was a brutal age. No one expected anything else.

One such band was the most brutal. They called themselves the Purifying Fire of the Goddess. Not the foolish goddess Sophia. No, these worshiped a Kali-like harpy with insatiable bloodlust. The altars they put up to Vengeance were hardly ever dry of the blood of the heretics.

Young Itzak had only just joined the Purifying Fire. He was a true believer in the Extinction. He didn't want to be like the others, who simply offered random old people and cripples to the insatiable goddess, pretending they were the servants of the scientist-priests. He wanted to find the true heretics.

It's hard to avoid seeing the hand of God's providence in such events, I think. You might call it luck. Or fortune of some kind, synchronicity.

However it was, Itzak happened to be sharing a meal with a family in an underground city, one of many such rabbit-warrens to be carved out in the past few years. And they told him a story of an old man with a golden hand.

Why didn't he simply think they were mad? Tribalism breeds superstition and the worst kinds of delusions. He knew this, even though he was young, not yet out of his teens. But there was something. A light in their eyes. A simultaneous fear, respect, nostalgia, replaced in the end by hatred.

He had seen that light before. It was the mark of the philosopher-kings. The heretics.

So he listened. They led him to a secret place, deeper and darker even than the cities.

It was a natural cavern of crystal. Amethyst, coral, pale gold—colors he had not even known existed— danced as soon as he entered with his torch. In the middle of the cavern was a column, where, uncounted ages before man even walked the surface, a stalactite met a stalagmite. At the midpoint of that meeting, a thin filigree of bone-like calcium, hung a simple wooden cross.

Kneeling before it was an old man, all hair and beard.

He smiled at Itzak, even as he extended his hands to be bound.

KONTAKION THREE

By the power of the Holy Spirit doth each blossom breathe with fragrance: it gives forth its exquisite scent, shows its delicate color, and reveals the beauty of the Great in the tiniest of things. Praise and honor to the life-giving God who spreads out the meadows like a carpet of flowers, how crowns the fields with the gold of wheat and the blue of cornflowers, and who crowns our souls with the joy of contemplation. Let us rejoice and sing to him: Alleluia!

THE WARRIORS of the Purifying Fire beat the old man, but not in fury. They were not like the marauders who picked off the weak at the dark edges of the underground cities. They were committed to the holy cause of Extinction. So their beating was a ritual, as was everything they did.

At the end of it, the old man was not quite unconscious, though clearly the worse for wear. Itzak looked at that face and wondered.

Here was a man who had held power in his hands that the gods would be jealous of. Here was a man who had controlled the destiny of millions. Here was a man who could summon fire from the bowels of the earth itself.

A weak, bleeding, pitiful splinter of humanity.

Who smiled, in spite of the pain.

Itzak hated him.

But that night, Itzak couldn't sleep. He kept seeing Abram's face as it was during the beatings. He had no word to describe it, for the emotions in the old man's eyes were entirely foreign to him. If he had lived in a different age, he might have used a word like beatific. In his limited experience, he assumed it was some act of magical protection. After all, the others had squealed like pigs during the beatings.

Finally, he couldn't stand it any more.

Checking to see that the rest of his brothers were asleep, he crawled to the immovable body of the old man.

At first, he only stared. But the righteous anger welled up inside him, as it often did. He kicked the old man.

A soft grunt, and the matted hair and beard turned over to look at Itzak.

"Come to finish the job?" the old man asked, a smile at the corners of his eyes.

"You are responsible for the death of billions," demanded Itzak. "For the loss of all that was beautiful on the surface. Why is that pain not etched on your face?"

The smile faded, a little. Itzak was pleased.

"The earth is a garden," said the old man. "Now is simply a long winter. All winters pass."

"You are a fool," said Itzak. "This is the winter of extinction."

"What do they teach the children these days?" the old man tut-tutted. "Bad stories, that's what. Have you never heard the story of the Golden Tree?"

"Sounds like the worst sort of heresy," said Itzak, getting up to leave.

"Only to the craven," said the old man, suddenly very serious. "Listen now. You might learn something."

THE TALE of the Golden Tree

In simpler days, when the earth was younger, and the trees, the stones, the flowers were more alive than they are now, there was a land where humans lived in harmony with their surroundings.

In this land, a tribe of peaceful people farmed rich mountain-earth soils during the brilliant but short summers. The winters, though harsh, were warm with family-time by the fire. Children were conceived in winters. Children played outside in summers.

One of these children was the tribe's pride and joy. The youngest of the chief's many children, she had a peculiar mix of mischief and joy that endeared her to everyone. Living in a world of her own imagination, she would be up at the crack of dawn, insisting every one of her brothers and sisters accompany her out into a world of wonders.

She was the first to smell the lilies of the valley the morning they erupted from the black earth. She was the first to answer the geese's call as they returned each spring. She could sit on a boulder by the river, entranced by the play of sunlight on the ripples.

She even woke up some nights, as though the stars themselves spoke to her in hushed music.

And so, even though she poked and prodded her brothers and sisters until they could hardly stand it, they couldn't resent her. For the stillness of her face as she sat on a cliff contemplating the trees waving in the wind was almost adult in its intensity. And they loved her for it.

During a winter that lasted longer than seemed possible, the girl stepped to the threshold of womanhood. It should have been spring already, and so strange things awakened in her body. They should have been mirrored by the blossoming of the earth, but this winter simply did not end.

The girl's father, the chief, declared that there must be a great evil abroad. It must be purged before spring would come again. And he told his sons that whoever found and destroyed this evil would be chief of the tribe after him.

All this talk of great evils hardly concerned the young girl. How could she think of great evils when there were such scents on the breeze, when the distant mountains seemed to pierce the skin of heaven itself?

As she lay in the snow, muffled with furs, the sky opened to her, revealing itself as a great lake downside up. It made her dizzy, and she giggled. In such moments her heart was full with a sense that all was good and right, great evil or not.

But as the winter stretched on and on, the young woman grew restless. Something sang to her from the depths of the snow-covered forests. Or someone. Her mother and aunts warned her that it was the great evil calling to her. But she didn't believe them. One early morning, the song was too beautiful to ignore: it was tinged with something she never considered before. A joyful sadness.

She ran away. And there in the whispering forests she saw a wondrous being: a spirit-creature of wind and leaves and sunshine. A being wholly of this world, but also of another.

"Are you the great evil?" she asked it.

"I am not. I guard against it," the creature answered in song.

The girl ran away often in the early mornings. She reveled in the song of the spirit-guardian. In it, she remembered the dew on the petals of the daffodils, the colors of a spring sunrise, the blue on a hatching robin's egg. And she knew spring would come, no matter how long winter lasted.

One morning she stayed out longer than usual, urged on by a strange note in the Guardian's song. A sound that warned of danger. But adventure too.

And so she went further than she ever had before. All the way to the edge of land, where the sweet water turns salty. And there she saw an impossible thing. A mountain-like, shimmering mass of branchless trees, fluttering fabric, sprouting like weeds from a bowl of striped wood. She had no name for the thing it was—a ship.

But somehow she knew that nothing would ever be the same.

A second ship appeared on the horizon, and it peppered the first with fire that ripped it apart like a wolf feasting on a doe's belly. The first ship returned the favor. Amazed even as she was horrified, the girl watched it all. Her Guardian's song, usually so comforting, was silent, watchful, expectant.

Finally, nothing was left of either ship except floating wood and bloody bodies.

Led by her Guardian, the girl came to the shore of the sea. It was littered with the flotsam and jetsam of war.

Wood and flesh alike lay dead, except for one: a young man. He was alive, though barely.

The girl tended the wounded young man. She looked at him as he lay there, his skin white as milk, his hair red as fire. For a moment, she saw him only in the chaos of blood and foam that surrounded them.

Is this the great evil? She wondered, thinking of the horrors she had witnessed on the water.

Then he opened his eyes and looked at her, and all such thoughts fled. She saw the same restless hunger that she caught in her own eyes when she looked at her reflection in still pools. No, there was no evil here. There was something familiar, and warm, like a hearth in the middle of a winter snowstorm.

But then, her brothers came upon them. Seeing the carnage of battle, they said, "Behold, the great evil! Here is the reason for lingering winter. Hatred, and war, and man destroying the harmony of nature."

They dragged the young man back to the village. Their father the chief was greatly pleased. This young man's blood, he explained, would wash away the stain of the great evil. Spring would surely return.

But as her brothers stretched him out on the ground, the girl-child covered him with her own body.

"If you kill him," she said, "kill me as well. We are of the same tribe."

And in that moment, her Guardian came openly. The tribe was filled with terror at its song, and they fled. Only the young man remained with the girl.

"There is indeed a great evil in this land," said the Guardian. "An evil that can be beaten. Will you defeat it?"

There was much that the Guardian didn't say. But its song suggested more: loss and sadness, surely, but hope and love as well.

The young woman and the young man took each other's hands and walked into the unknown.

What they did not see, what they could not see, was that wherever their feet stepped, the snow melted. As they passed, snowdrops rose in their wake.

There was a mountain not far from there. The young woman's tribe called it the Old Man's Face. It did look very much like an old man, hoary with snow. But what a wonder: in the midst of all that snow grew a tree that shone gold in the twilight. It was covered in buds that threatened to sprout at any moment, as though stuck in time, waiting for a spring that wouldn't come. As the young man and woman came close, the tree was bathed in light.

The young woman gasped as she saw her Guardian bow before the tree and the light.

A voice spoke out of that light.

"Do you wish the evil to fade, and for spring to come again?"

"Yes," they said together.

"There is a way," said the voice in the light. "But it is a painful way. You can never return home. You must remain here until you die."

The girl looked around at the barrenness of that peak. She drew her fur cloak around her, but it did little to warm her. They would surely die before the coming of spring.

But at least spring *would* come.

"For my family," said the young woman.

"For the sins of my fathers," said the young man.

The Guardian sang in joy and grief mingled as he joined their hands together. And as they gave their word, the buds burst into white flowers. The snow receded, and look! They stood in a garden, filled with fruit trees and birds and small animals that came to them and nuzzled at their legs. The sun was warm on their faces, and their hearts were filled with love.

The spring came soon afterward, fed by the love of the young woman and the young man. It is said by many that their children's children still live there in a glorious city on a hill to this very day, and the cycle of seasons is the work of their love.

ITZAK FELT a strange stirring at the images evoked by the old man's tale. But it was a tale of the surface, of a world he had never seen with adult eyes. All he remembered were grays and browns and the fetid red of sickness.

And so, he scoffed at the old man's tale. A dreamer, that was all he was. A madman. It would be right and just to kill him.

As he fell asleep, he comforted himself with the thought:

May the old man's dreams end with him, and may Extinction come swiftly.

Ikos **Three**

How wondrous art thou in the triumph of spring, when every creature rises and joyfully greets thee in a thousand modes. Thou art the source of life, the destroyer of death. By the light of the moon nightingales sing, and the valleys and woods lie clad in a wedding garment white as snow. All the earth is thy promised pride awaiting her incorruptible Bridegroom. If the grass of the field is clothed in this way, how gloriously shalt thou transfigure us in the future age of the resurrection! How splendid our bodies shall be, how radiant our souls!

Glory to thee, bringing up from the dark depths of the earth

An endless variety of colors, tastes, and scents.

Glory to thee for the warmth and tenderness of the natural world.

Glory to thee for the thousands of creatures thou hast placed all around us.

Glory to thee for the depths of thine understanding, whose seal thou hast stamped all the world.

Glory to thee: I reverently kiss the traces of thy invisible steps.

Glory to thee, kindling before us the clear light of eternal life.

Glory to the for the hope of the ideal, imperishable beauty of immortality.

Glory to thee, O God, from age to age!

ABRAM WAS DISTURBED by the young man Itzak. He had seen many of the warrior caste in his days. They all had a light in their eyes, a light of furious purpose. The same light that heretics and revolutionaries had as they burned, tied to stakes. But this young man had a different light in his eyes. He was aflame with righteous anger; he desired justice, not revenge.

What a tragedy that he had no other way to follow, except the way of the warriors for extinction!

That thought grew inside Abram, not letting him sleep, niggling at the corners of his mind. It had been a long time since he had prayed. Truly prayed. For he had long ago lost hope.

But now, something like an ember came alight inside him. He gathered his aching body together and rose up onto bony knees racked with pains old and new. He looked up at the ceiling of rock. Somewhere far, far beyond it there was sky and sun, or perhaps the perfection of the stars.

Then, he prayed. He prayed like he had not prayed in years. There were hardly any words in that prayer, only a rising wave of... something.

He was shocked to put a name to that emotion rising within him.

It was gratitude.

Glory to thee, it said. For this moment especially. For the pain, for the tragedy. For *now*.

And then, something strange happened. A light appeared as though out of nowhere. It hovered like a bright mist above him. At first, he couldn't understand it. His rational mind did its best to intervene.

An anomaly. A chemical reaction, perhaps. A reflection of a sunrise through a deep chasm of rock.

But his heart told him a different story. This was the light of the Golden Tree. Even here in the tomb of humanity.

The light faded, leaving an imprint like fire on his memory.

Spring would come again, he know. And he knew what he must do.

. . .

Kontakion Four

How thou dost delight them that contemplate thee! How life-giving thy holy Word! Converse with thee is smoother than oil and sweeter than the honeycomb. Prayer before thee lifts up and enlivens. And then, what trembling fills the soul! How majestic nature becomes; how clearly in points to thee! Where thou art not, there is only emptiness; where thou art, the soul is filled with abundance, and the song resounds in a living torrent: Alleluia!

Ikos Four

When evening comes over the earth, when the peace of the night's sleep and the silence of the spent day reigns, then in the splendor of the sun's declining rays, filtering through the clouds, I see the image of thy bridal chamber. The fire and porphyry, the gold and sapphire speak prophet-like concerning the ineffable beauty of thy dwellings, and they call out in triumph: 'Let us go the Father.'

Glory to thee at the hushed hour of night.

Glory to thee, pouring out thy peace upon the world.

Glory to thee for the last ray of the setting sun.

Glory to thee for the rest of a grace-filled sleep.

Glory to thee for thy goodness even in the time of darkness when all the world is hidden from our eyes.

Glory to thee for the fervent prayers offered by a trembling soul.

Glory to thee for the pledge of our reawakening to joy
On that eternal Day that knows no evening.

Glory to thee, O God, from age to age.

UNBEKNOWNST TO ABRAM, Itzak was awake, staring at his charge through the night. When the old man started to get up, Itzak's hand reached for his knife, always handy under the cloak he used as a pillow. But the old fool was only performing some ritual.

Then, something odd happened. A light appeared out of nowhere. It was misty, even milky, not quite distinct unless you looked slightly away from it and allowed the peripheral vision to dominate.

And it seemed to settle directly on the head and shoulders of the old man.

Then, it turned into gold radiance for a moment, as though the rocks above that served instead of a sky were rent apart, and the sun pierced through for a brilliant moment.

Itzak was terrified. This was some foul magic of the priest-kings. This was an invocation of the same spirit that had brought the whole world down.

He wanted to throw his knife, but something stopped him. He tried to convince himself it wasn't terror. Terror that killing a magician in the middle of his incantation would somehow cause the magic to rebound on him, turning him into something horrible. Or killing him outright.

So he lay still, forcing his terror down, watching the old man.

He promised himself he would kill the old man himself

tomorrow. Forget the ritual sacrifice. This old man was too dangerous.

Kontakion Five

The dark storm clouds of life bring no terror to those in whose hearts thy lamp is burning brightly. Outside is darkness and rain, the terror and howling of the storm, but in the soul, in the presence of Christ, there is light and peace—silence. The heart sings: Alleluia!

Ikos Five

I see thy heavens glistening with stars. How rich thou art, how much light is thine! Eternity watches me by the rays of the distant stars. I am small, insignificant, but the Lord is with me. Thy loving right hand keeps me everywhere and always.

Glory to thee, ceaselessly watching over me.

Glory to thee for my providential meetings with other people.

Glory to thee for the love of family,

For the faithfulness of friends.

Glory to thee for the meekness of the animals who serve me.

Glory to thee for the bright moments of my life.

Glory to thee for the innocent joy of the heart.

Glory to thee for the happiness of living and moving and having our being in thee.

Glory to thee, O God, from age to age.

In the morning, Itzak awoke Abram before anyone else was up. He woke him up with the point of his knife against the old man's jugular.

"You were performing vile magic last night, weren't you? Where is your shame? You brought destruction to the earth, and yet you persist in it?"

The old man, to his credit, was very still as the knife-point slowly bored itself into flesh.

"It wasn't anything *I* did, young man. It was the light of the Golden Tree."

Itzak laughed. But he didn't retract the point of the knife.

"You amuse me, old man. There are no trees left."

The old man looked at him for a long time, then turned away. When he began speaking, it was as though he was talking to the stones and the dirt under his feet, not to Itzak.

The Shadow People

In simpler days, when the earth was young, and the trees, the stones, the flowers were more alive than they are now, there was a land where humans lived in harmony with their surroundings.

This highland was set apart from the lowland, a city upon a hill, covered with great houses and streets that seemed paved with gold in the light of the setting sun. At the heart of this city was a true wonder of the world: a tree that seemed to give off its own golden light. By the light of this tree, the city prospered.

The people of that city understood that the lowlands were dark and fallen, and they were only protected from that corruption by the tree that grew in their midst. And so, every child remembered their first warning as gospel truth: never, never go beyond the light of the tree.

In this city, there lived a curious girl. The girl loved the tree, and she loved her city, of course she did! The light was comforting, the flowers fragrant, and the people kind. But she liked much more the shapes of shadows formed by the light against stones and blades of grass. There was a murmuring life in those shadows, a secret excitement.

And she noticed, naturally, that the further she wandered from the tree, the larger, more exciting the shadows.

But the most wonderful shadow of all was the night sky, a field plowed with stars. Every evening she sat deep into the night, staring up, giving thanks for how small she was, and how great the stars were, and how right the darkness between the stars was. And sometimes, on rare occasions, rabbits and foxes and marmots would join her. For those moments, it seemed the old harmony between man and nature was restored.

One night, a storm struck the mountain. Rain fell in sheets that sparkled like liquid diamonds in the lightning. Thunder boomed in words that seemed almost another language. Most amazing were the shadows cast back by the flash of fire from the sky.

But nothing could have prepared the girl for what she saw next. The lightning and the light of the tree mingled in a moment that seemed to burn into the backs of her eyes. In that flashing shadow, she saw the image of the tree against a distant mountain-top. It was a hundred times greater in size and complexity, the branches whorled into patterns that suggested artifice, not nature. And it seemed to her that a fountain of gold burst from the trunk and filled the sky with stars.

All her family hid from the storm in their houses, but the girl remained rooted to the spot, staring at the darkness where she had just seen a miracle: a creation of shadow and light, more spectacular than both.

In that vision, she heard singing. A choir of voices that sounded human, but she understood neither the words nor the music. She thought if she could only focus on its joyful sadness long enough, she would understand it. It made her want to weep and laugh at the same time. It ripped at her heart and filled her chest with light.

All the next day, she pondered her vision. But no one could tell her what it meant.

Kontakion Six

How great and how close art thou in the powerful track of the storm! How mighty thy right arm in the blinding flash of the lightning! How wonderful thy greatness! The voice of the Lord is heard over the fields; it speaks in the rustling of the trees. The voice of the Lord is in the crash of the thunder and the downpour; the voice of the Lord is upon many waters. Praise be to thee in the roar of mountains ablaze. Thou dost shake out the earth like a garment; the waves of the sea dost thou pile up to heaven. Praise be to thee, humbling the pride of man and rousing in him a cry of penitence: Alleluia!

Ikos **Six**

When the lightning flash has lit up the hall of feasting, how feeble seems the light from the lantern. And thou, like the lightning, dost unexpectedly flash in my soul at the time of life's most intense joys. After the brightness of thy lightning flash, how drab, how colorless, how illusory all else seems! And so my soul cleaves to thee.

GLORY TO THEE, the furthest bound and limit of man's dreaming.

Glory to thee for our unquenchable thirst for fellowship with God.

Glory to thee, inspiring in us dissatisfaction with earthly things.

Glory to thee, bathing us in thy subtle rays.

Glory to thee, subduing the power of the spirits of darkness

And condemning every evil to naught.

Glory to thee for thy revelation,

For the happiness of perceiving thee and living with thee.

Glory to thee, O God, from age to age!

THE MUSIC that the young girl heard haunted her. It seemed to urge her to a life she couldn't yet imagine. Then she looked at the simple ways of her people, and she was unsat-isfied. More than that, she started to ask difficult questions. What was the source of her people's prosperity? How could it be that this place alone was blessed, while all the rest of the lands were cursed? Were her people more virtuous than all others? Certainly that could not be true. Were all the nations of the lowlands, then, guilty of some terrible evil that her people managed to avoid?

She wanted to believe that. It seemed many of her fellows believed it. But her heart rebuked her. Such thoughts rang false, especially when compared to the heart-rending truth of the music.

And so, further and further she came to the edges of the tree's light. She walked in every direction, unbothered by crag or by precipice. Everywhere she searched for some-thing; everywhere she hoped to hear that choir again.

Kontakion Seven

In the wondrous blending of sounds it is thy call we hear. In the harmony of many voices, in the sublime beauty of music, in the glory of the works of great composers, thou art there showing us the threshold of the paradise that is to come. All true beauty has the power to draw the soul towards thee, and to make it sing in ecstasy: Alleluia!

One night, she was awoken by the music. All her family were asleep, and she stole out quietly. The music was like a fragrance hugging the tips of the wind: barely there, but intense in the experience. One moment it was a single, sad voice, another it was a choir of such joyful sadness, she found tears pouring down her cheeks. And always the sound came from the shadows.

She stopped by a narrow cave that looked completely black in the night. Only the edges of the cave's stone walls sparkled in the light of the golden tree. She was sure the music was coming from there.

"Come out!" she whispered urgently. "Teach me your song, so we can sing it together."

A shadowy creature moved in the darkness.

"We are not allowed to come to you," a boy spoke with a ringing voice. "We must not leave the shadows."

"And I must not leave the light. What are we to do?"

That silence seemed pregnant with voices on the brink of singing.

"I know!" said the girl, suddenly inspired. "You reach out your hands to me, and I'll reach out my hands to you. We'll meet halfway."

The hands that reached out to her were scarred, covered with calluses. They seemed the hands of an old man. But the voice was that of a boy.

"Who are you?" he asked. "Why are you speaking to us?"

"Why shouldn't I?" she asked.

"You're not allowed," he answered. "You're the people of the tree. We're the people of the shadows."

And he told her the story of his people. They were a gifted race, with deft abilities of handiwork, invention, and music. They came from a distant land, where they lived simply, not unlike the people of the tree. But invasion stormed their shores, and they were taken by lowlanders as spoils of war. Brought into the lowlands under the city on a hill, they soon became sought-after for their talents. Even the people of the tree came to covet the artifice of the people of the shadows.

"But why do you not come and live with us, then?" asked the girl.

"We are not allowed," was all he said. "You are the people of the tree. We're the people of the shadows."

As soon as he said that, the girl realized that she had just about had it with taboos. With a furtive look at the tree, she jumped into the shadows.

Ikos Seven

Catching them up in the Holy Spirit, like the dawn thou dost break over the thought of artists and poets and the great minds of science. By the power of thy supreme knowledge they prophetically comprehend thy laws, descrying for us the depths of thy creative wisdom. Their works speak unwittingly of thee. How great art thou in thy creation! How great art thou in man!

Glory to thee, manifesting thine inconceivable power in the laws of the universe.

Glory to thee, for all nature is filled with thy laws.

Glory to thee for all thou hast revealed to us in thy mercy.

Glory to thee for all thou hast hidden from us in thy wisdom.

Glory to thee for the genius of the human mind.

Glory to thee for the dignity of man's labor.

Glory to thee for the fiery tongues
That bring inspiration.
Glory to Thee, O God, from age to age!

IN THE SHADOWS, the girl found a new world. The people of the shadows were talented in ways she could hardly imagine. Everything they touched seemed filled with grace. And the music they made on their instruments and with their voices was unlike anything she had ever heard. But all of it was imbued with sorrow so profound she could not hear it without weeping.

"I don't understand," she finally said. "Why are you not allowed into the light of the tree?"

"You may regret knowing," said her new friend, the boy.

But she insisted. So he took her to an old woman with canny eyes.

"Show her, grandma," he said.

The old woman took the girl to a crack in the cave wall where the light of the tree streamed in. As soon as she walked into the light, she was no longer an old woman, but a vibrant young creature with flowing hair and eyes like diamonds. She shone with light that was not merely a reflection of the tree, but was its own creation. And the girl thought of the vision she had seen, where the light of the tree and the shadows came together to create something more beautiful than both.

"You are beautiful," she said to the old woman.

The woman smiled sadly. "What you see is not what I am. This is the curse of our people. In the light of the tree, I reflect *your* true self."

The girl blushed. But then, the full truth came to her.

"Those who have secret sins, those whose inner life is corrupt: what do they see when they look at you?"

The old woman nodded. "What they see is horrible."

And the full and dark truth of the city on a hill dawned on the girl.

All her people were content to use the artifice of the enslaved people of the shadows. But they dared not allow the people into the city, for then the truth of their own hearts would be manifest before their eyes.

She looked at the people with new eyes. Now she saw their sunken, sallow faces, their calloused hands, the marks of whips on their shoulders and necks. And a great need rose up inside her.

Kontakion Eight

How near thou art in days of sickness and pain. Thou thyself dost visit the sick; thou thyself dost stoop beside the sufferer's bed, and his heart doth converse with thee. In the throes of sorrow and suffering thou bringest peace and unexpected consolation. Thou dost comfort; thou art the Love that tries men's hearts and saves them. To thee we sing the song: Alleluia!

The old woman of the shadow-people, it turned out, was a protector of runaways. With her were fifty of her people who had been slaves in the lowlands. They had only stopped by the city on the hill to see the light of the tree before their journey, a last glimpse of hope before an uncertain future.

But the girl had a different idea. There were many caves and hidden places in the mountains around the city. Enough to hold many hundreds for a short time, until she could persuade her own people to let the people of the shadows into the city.

The old woman and the girl struck a bargain, and their great work began. Over the next days and weeks a network of tunnels and caves and secret roads was charted out, and a movement of runaways began, led by the grandmother and the girl. Their dangers were many, and some didn't make it. But many more did.

It could not last. Word of the runaway network reached the lowland nations. They gathered a great army, which surrounded the mountain and the city on a hill. And the people of the tree turned on the girl and her charges.

"You have brought a great evil upon us! You have broken the word of our forefathers. And now our city will perish."

The people of the tree were not warriors. They had no way of withstanding the might of the lowlanders. And so, the city fell. In a blaze of fury, the armies tore up buildings and roads alike. Last of all, they came for the tree. They felled it, hacking it into pieces, as though it were the source of all the world's woes.

But the girl and the old woman escaped with the remainder of the shadow people. And with them, they took a fruit of the tree, and disappeared into the shadows.

Sometimes, on stormy nights, you can still hear them singing.

THE OLD MAN FELL SILENT.

But Itzak was incensed. "That is not how that tale ends, is it?"

Abram lowered his eyes and shook his head.

"Tell me the end of it!" demanded Itzak.

The old man said nothing.

"Then I will offer my own. That city on a hill that you have described turned into a bastion, not of wisdom and civilization, but of corruption, slavery, and injustice. All its good intentions were false, for all the gold, all the light, all the apparent beauty brought from the lowlands was furrowed on the back of slavery. Of intolerance. Of inequality."

The old man remained silent.

"Can we trust this civilization if it was built on the backs of slaves? I say to you: no!"

"But there was so much beauty, and there were so many good people, and so much potential, so much..."

"No! I reject it all. The experiment failed. Time to chuck it out."

Itzak left Abram alive and went back to his brothers.

Abram felt that perhaps it would have been better if Itzak had killed him. What if everything that Itzak said was true? What if the brief appearances of light and beauty were worth nothing because of the corruption and sin that pervades all of man's doings? Was not the poisoning of the Earth itself the greatest proof of this?

Abram looked up, hoping to see the light again. But he saw only the stones of the underland, their tomb.

Ikos Eight

When in childhood I called upon thee consciously for the first time, thou didst fulfill my prayer and overshadow my heart with reverent peace. At that moment I understood: thou art good, and blessed are those who turn to thee in prayer. I began to call upon thee again and again, and even now I cry out:

GLORY TO THEE, satisfying my desires with good things.

Glory to thee, keeping vigil over me day and night.

Glory to thee, treating pain and loss with the healing passage of time.

Glory to thee, with whom there is no grief without hope, O Giver of life to all.

Glory to thee, who has made immortal all that is lofty and good

And who dost promise us that longed-for meeting with those who have died.

Glory to thee, O God, from age to age!

KONTAKION **Nine**

How is it that, on a feast day, the whole of nature mysteriously smiles? How is it that a wonderful lightness is spilled out in our hearts, a lightness that cannot be compared with anything earthly, and the very air in the church and in the altar becomes luminous? This is the breathing of thy grace; this is the reflection of Tabor's light. Then heaven and earth sing thy praise: Alleluia!

· · ·

Ikos Nine

When thou didst inspire me to serve my neighbors and didst fill my soul with humility, then did one of thy number-less rays of light fall upon my heart, making it luminous, like iron glowing in the furnace. I have seen thy face: elusive and full of mystery.

GLORY TO THEE, transfiguring our lives with virtuous deeds.

Glory to thee, sealing ineffable pleasure in each of thy commandments.

Glory to thee, clearly abiding with us wherever the sweet scent of mercy wafts.

Glory to thee, sending us failure and misfortune that we may understand the suffering of others.

Glory to thee, making good to be its own reward within us.

Glory to thee, welcoming the impulse of the feeling of our heart.

Glory to thee, exalting love beyond all things
That are in heaven or on earth.

Glory to thee, O God, from age to age!

THE NEXT MORNING, the band of warriors reached the most dangerous part of their journey. Ever since the explosion of Yucca Mountain, the earth slept fitfully. She would some-times have nightmares, and the results on her children were catastrophic. Quakes that would bury entire underground cities in an instant. Tremors that destroyed passageways and storehouses essential for survival.

One such nightmare had plugged the underground road leading to the place of sacrifice. Some of the warriors had impiously suggested that another place of sacrifice could easily be prepared. But the leader of the warriors understood the importance of the site, if they did not. He would not listen to them. He even executed one of them merely for suggesting it.

But this meant that this sacrifice required the unthinkable: that the entire band go aboveground for a harrowing fifteen minutes. Usually, that left them shaken and terrified, but with symptoms that faded after mere days of discomfort.

However, if mother earth below was a fitful sleeper, above ground she was a raging tyrant. Every time they came up, the landscape was different. New hills, new fissures, new scars in the bones and skin of the earth. So it was with the same trepidation that they always approached the stairs that led them back up, away from the huddling comfort of the underlands.

This time was no different. More than that, Itzak was struck with a sense of purpose and significance that sometimes came over him. A kind of prophetic intuition. Something was going to happen. And it wasn't going to be good.

They had only been in the upper lands a few minutes when clouds gathered, so quickly that it seemed like sorcery. Itzak knew that he had been right. If it rained on them, then most of them would die. He had no words for the pestilence that came down from the sky. Abram did. He whispered, "Acid rain." Pulling his cloak over his head, he wrapped himself in his own bony embrace.

The rain struck them only minutes from the fissure that

led them back down. But when they came there, it was blocked. Immediately, half the warriors were taken by a frenzy of recrimination, blaming each other and their leader for what they now knew would be their inevitable death. Even as they thrashed about under the burning rain, the welts on their skin ripened like unholy fruit.

Itzak was disgusted with them. Throwing off his outer clothing, he reached under the boulder that wedged the entrance shut. It budged. He gathered every ounce of strength he had, and the fissure opened like the mouth of snoring man.

They all hurried in, jostling Abram ahead of them. Itzak was last to come down, and as he slipped in, the boulder shuddered and fell, closing the fissure completely.

There was no way back home, now. They would perform the final ritual, and they would die.

It was fitting, Itzak thought. But it was his last thought. He collapsed and knew no more.

Kontakion Ten

No one can restore what has crumbled into dust, but thou canst restore a conscience turned to ashes. Thou cants restore to its former beauty a soul whose beauty is hopelessly lost. With thee, there is nothing that cannot be made right. Thou art all love. Thou art Maker and Restorer. We praise thee with the song: Alleluia!

The warriors, unwilling to leave behind one of their own, rested to await Itzak's fate. That night would determine whether or not he survived. Even if he did survive, he would be little more than a husk of his former self.

So they all lay down where they were—in a long downward-sloping corridor of jagged flint. Abram alone did not fall asleep. He waited for the rest of the warriors to doze off, and then he pulled a small vial out of his cloak pocket. It was filled with a brown, creamy liquid of his own making. Gently, tenderly, he salved the skin of Itzak, which was now riddled with angry, red mounds. Itzak moaned, resisting him, but then he relaxed into the old man's touch, like a baby comforted by its mother.

When Abram finished, he knew Itzak would survive. Already the red had subsided, and Itzak's breathing had deepened and lost its sickly rattle.

In the middle of the night, Itzak cried out in fear and woke up. He saw that his skin was unusually firm, and the welts had already receded more than he thought possible. Abram lay at his feet, comfortably sleeping.

For the first time, Itzak saw the old man as Abram. Not as *heretic*, not as *abomination*, not as *other*. As himself. And in that moment, he realized that Abram had healed him. That thought left a gurgling emptiness in his chest that started to seethe like an angry snake.

He woke the old man up urgently, filled with a need to thank him. But he had no words. Abram seemed to understand, though. He smiled.

"I will tell you the end of the tale, if you will hear it," Abram said.

Itzak nodded.

. . .

The Tale of the False Tree

In latter days, when the earth was old, and the trees, the stones, the flowers seemed more real from a safe distance, there was a land where humans lived in comfort, safe from their surroundings.

They lived in perfect happiness. They never fell ill, all they could ever want was at the tips of their fingers, and money was no object. The best food, the most comfortable clothing, the most luxurious and elaborate entertainments: they had it all.

In this perfect land lived a young man. Like all of his friends, he enjoyed the goods of his life. He lived largely, ate extravagantly, and loved much.

But one evening, a storm hit that land, tearing apart the sky with lightning. The young man, enchanted, walked outside to watch. In the spaces between the thunder's roars, the young man thought he heard something else. It was faint, barely there. It took him a long time to place that sound, though it was so familiar that it made him ache with nostalgia. Then he realized: it was a choir. Sorrowful singing, filled with quiet joy, in a language he hardly understood, except that the meaning seemed just on the tip of his tongue. For the first time in his memory, the young man wept.

From that day on, every evening he remembered the pain of that song, and he wept again. More often than not, he would fall asleep, still weeping.

To his own shock and surprise, he didn't resent the pain, as his rational mind told him he should. No, he was grateful for it. His heart told him that the pain was its own reward, though he hardly understood how or why.

Still, every morning, the pain seemed little more than an afterthought, and he couldn't help but forget it with riotous living and beautiful friends and lovers.

One evening, as he sat on his porch and wept, he saw a strange sight. An old woman, dressed in rags, dirty and disheveled, walked by his house. The young man had never seen anyone poor like her, and for a moment his curiosity overcame everything.

Then he noticed that the old woman was limping, and he felt sorry for her.

"Where are you going, old woman?" he asked. "Perhaps I can help you get there."

The old woman accepted the young man's help willingly. They walked together for some time in silence, until they arrived at a hut in the woods, so old it was barely standing.

"Thank you, young man," said the old woman. "Will you accept a gift from me in payment for your kindness?"

"Oh, I don't need anything, old woman. I have everything I could ever ask for."

"Is that so?" said the old woman. "Then why do you weep every night?"

"How do you know about that?"

"Can you keep a secret?" the old woman asked with a wink. "I am a healer, and I think I have just the medicine for you, if you want it. But it is a bitter pill to swallow."

The young man laughed. "You don't frighten me, old woman."

"Very well," she said, and waved her hand.

Immediately, the young man found himself in a different place: a sterile, concrete hall lit with sickly yellow lights. All around him, lined up in perfect intervals and spaces, were hundreds upon hundreds of beds, filled with sleeping people of all ages, sizes, and colors. To his horror, he knew one of the sleepers. He recognized himself.

"What is this, a nightmare?" he asked the old woman.

"No, my child," said the old woman. "This is the awakening."

In the humming, dreadful un-silence of that hall of sleepers, the old woman continued, "Let me tell you a story of your world."

There once was a mighty kingdom, governed by a great king who wished his people to be the happiest and most content subjects of any kingdom in the world. But this presented him with an impossible challenge. For the world was a harsh place. There was only so much food to go around, and the threat of bad harvests was constant. War and pestilence was a shadow looming on the horizon at all times. And no matter how wisely he ruled, there would still be some who rebelled, who took advantage of others, who murdered and raped and pillaged.

He wondered about this problem; he pondered it all the hours of the day. He grew old and weary, thinking of it. Until one day, a stranger came into his court.

This stranger claimed to have an answer to the king's dilemma. He claimed the knowledge to make the king's subjects the happiest and most content of any land. But the knowledge came at a price.

"Name it," said the king, "and though it be three-quarters of my kingdom, I will give it to you."

The stranger smiled a twisted smile, and he said, "In a manner of speaking, three-quarters is exactly what I require."

And he gave the king the knowledge. When the king found

out what it was, he was grieved. For three-quarters of his kingdom was a heavy price to pay. But for the sake of the one quarter that he could save from danger, unhappiness, and a life of uncertainty, he agreed.

With the help of the stranger's knowledge, the king built a mighty tree of metal and wheels. With dark magic, this tree fed on the earth itself to create fruits of charmed sweetness. Every person who ate one of these fruits fell into an enchanted sleep and entered a shared dream world. In this dream world, there was no sickness, no political hatred, no war. It was a perfect collective. But there were only so many fruits to go around. And so, only one quarter of the king's people received the precious fruits of the collective.

The king bore a great burden of guilt. For the remaining three quarters of his kingdom that he gave to the stranger suffered greatly. The stranger took all of them and made them slaves of the false tree, for it was a complicated machine, requiring constant maintenance. At night, they were herded into camps, kept safe by barbed wire and machine guns. And the people groaned under the heaviness of their new taskmaster, the stranger.

The King grieved for them. But he knew that this was the price of utopia. So, he left the sleepers to their enchanted sleep, and the slaves to their toil and drudgery.

Ikos 10

Thou knowest, my God, the fall of the angel Lucifer, full of pride: save me by the power of thy grace. Grant me not to fall away from thee; grant me never to doubt thee. Sharpen my hearing that I may hear thy mysterious voice every minute of my life and may call upon thee, who are every-where present:

GLORY to thee for the timing of every circumstance.

Glory to thee for what thou speakest in my heart.

Glory to thee for the command of thy mysterious voice.

Glory to thee for thy revelations that come both when I sleep and when I wake.

Glory to thee for unraveling our vain designs.

Glory to thee for shaking us free of passion's frenzy through our experience of suffering.

Glory to thee for humbling the pride of our heart

For the sake of our salvation.

Glory to thee, O God, from age to age!

THE OLD WOMAN finished her tale. The young man was horrified.

"What sort of medicine is this? It makes my heart groan with even greater pain!"

"It is necessary, my boy," she said, and reached into her tattered cloak.

She pulled out a crystal globe that radiated a golden light. In that unearthly glow of the humming off-white lights, it looked like a sunrise. For a moment, the young man was mesmerized, seeing nothing but dancing lights. But his vision cleared, and he saw what was inside. It was a tiny sapling covered in buds that looked ready to burst at any moment.

As he looked into it, he heard the music again, faint as a

memory. It grew, but inside him, as though the source of the sound was his own heart. His entire being filled with light and music. It hurt. But the pain was a greater pleasure than his entire life had been up to this moment.

"This life you live is a lie, my boy," said the old woman. "Your joy is false, for it is built on the suffering of the outcast. I lived that way once, too, as a child. But I could not bear to live at the expense of the suffering of others. There is another way. Once, long ago, I lived in a city upon a hill. A place where man and nature lived in harmony."

"What happened to it?" asked the young man.

"It was destroyed by the ancestors of your king. But the hope of my city on the hill remains."

She raised the globe, and the light grew, until the pasty, slack faces of the sleepers gathered color and life. Some of them even began to stir to slight wakefulness.

"This sapling is all that remains of the promise of the city on the hill. As long as it exists, hope remains."

The song rose again inside the young man, and he realized that he could never again return to his former life.

"Can anything be done?" he asked. "I want to help."

The old woman smiled sadly. "Yes, you can help, my boy. But you will have to go back to sleep to do it."

In spite of the horror, the young man knew his answer before he spoke it.

"I am ready," said the young man.

The young man woke up in his empty bed, in his empty house, in his empty life. He wanted to weep, but he didn't. For on the table by his bed stood the crystal globe with the sapling. And the music, he realized, was still inside him, rising and falling like his own breathing.

From that moment, his life changed. No longer did he seek pleasures. Instead, he sought souls.

At first, he didn't know what to do. To his shock, he realized that most of his friends hardly even looked him in the eye. Before this moment, he had never before sought the contact of another's eyes.

One by one, he caught the eyes of his friends. He began to tell them stories. Stories of a legendary city, of people living in shadows, of songs that could cut your heart open. Everywhere he went, he carried the sapling with him. As he spoke of the music, the sapling sang into the hearts of those ready to listen. And more and more of his friends began to wake up.

With each awakening, the dream world crumbled. The colors faded. The joys rang hollow. The pleasures turned to ashes in the sleepers' mouths.

It could not remain thus for long, the young man knew. One evening, as he was telling a story to the largest group yet, the soldiers of the king came and arrested him.

He was charged with treason and sedition, and he was sentenced to death. But not just any death. He was to be an example for all who would try to emulate him. For his execution, every single sleeper was awakened.

All the people of that land, sleeper and slave alike, were gathered at the foot of the great tree of metal and wheels. The young man was hanged on the branches of the tree, impaled on its sharp edges.

Most of the sleepers jeered at him, cursing him for awakening them into this wasteland of a life, away from their perpetual pleasures. Those sleepers whom he had awakened to the deep life remained silent, afraid for their own skins. The slaves did not even dare to look up, for fear that they would join him, for that tree of metal was wide and tall, and many were the thorns ripe for impaling.

As the young man hung there, the king himself took the crystal globe and raised it high, for everyone to see.

And the young man saw the old woman in the crowd. But in the light of the tree, her face was young. And the young man's heart filled with love.

The king looked at the young man, and his face twisted with anger.

"Look at your hope, young man. This is all it is good for!"

He shattered the crystal at the foot of the tree. The sapling, he trampled into the dust.

"What was the point?" demanded the king. "You could have been blissful, even in ignorance."

But the young man didn't curse his king.

He thanked him: "I have had the greatest joys: the touch of love in service to my people. It is a painful thing, but it is a far, far greater thing than your illusions. And to die for that love? It is fitting. I thank you for it."

The young man died, impaled on the tree. But in death, his face was beautiful.

They left him hanging there. The king wanted all to see as the ravens pecked his eyes out and the carrion birds feasted on his flesh. But no living thing touched him. Then night fell, and all the people hurried back to their lives: the sleepers to their bliss, and the slaves to their camps.

That night, snow fell for the first time in many years. It sparkled like diamonds in the moonlight.

No one, not even the king, noticed that the remnants of

the sapling, bathed in the man's blood, had taken root and begun to grow.

All through the night, the sapling grew. Its supple bark wove itself in between the twisted barbs and shards of the false, metal tree. It grew faster than any tree had ever grown, as though a lifetime had been compressed into a single night. And the branches wove a bed for the young man, gently lifting him off the thorns impaling him, into a cocoon of leaves and buds and branches.

As the sun rose, the false tree groaned with agony, for the living tree was tearing it apart. The slaves fled in terror, ignoring the whips of their taskmasters. All the sleepers came suddenly awake again. They demanded that the king do something, that he destroy the living, breathing tree that had uprooted their dreamscape.

The king ordered that it be chopped down. But the tree continued to grow, and two new branches sprung up for every one that the king's henchmen hacked off.

"Burn it!" screamed the king. "Quickly!"

And they did. The tree burned like kindling, the fire running up the entire length and breadth of the tree as if it were coated with oil. But then, something strange happened. The tree burned, but it was not consumed. Only the outer bark crackled and twisted in the flames. Underneath was a silvery bark that gave off a light of its own, mingling with the dancing flames to create a kaleidoscope of color. Then, in a single moment, all the buds of the tree exploded in the flames. The burning tree was surrounded by a fountain of golden pollen that rose and rose and rose, until the sky over the entire country was filled with it.

The tree continued to burn, until the metal it had

become intertwined with melted, until every single fruit of the false tree withered and died, until there was not a trace left of the abomination of the stranger. Then, the golden tree itself burned. It left nothing behind, not even the body of the young man.

With the destruction of the metal tree, the bliss of the dreamscape was destroyed. The slaves were set free, and the sleepers returned to their lives as they were. The king died soon after, and all the uncertainty, pain, and sorrow that he had sought to destroy returned.

One morning, every citizen of that country was surprised to find a golden sapling growing in their gardens. It gave off a soft light, and if you looked at it for a long time, you had the distinct impression that there was a choir singing a very sad song somewhere far away.

The people of that land were tense and watchful, not knowing what this sign meant.

But the friends of the young man whom he had awakened recognized what this was. It was their time. They remembered their friend, the young man, and they were grateful for his gift. They traveled from house to house, telling the stories of the city on a hill, the people of the shadow, and the light of the golden tree.

And slowly, but surely, the people saw the beauty of their world again. They smelled the lilac on the breeze, they heard the call of the loon, and they stayed up late to see the night sky. And there, in the darkness between the stars, they heard a sorrowful music calling them home.

· · ·

ITZAK WAS SHELLSHOCKED. The story was like prophecy. Did Abram know the warriors were taking him to a place where a dead tree stood, to crucify him on that tree?

For the first time, he doubted his calling. He doubted the need for extinction.

But he was deprived of speech completely by the words of Abram that followed.

"Forgive me, Itzak. Forgive me for causing the death of the world, for cutting short your future. I accept my guilt and my just execution. Do not fear to do what you are called to do. I am a fitting sacrifice for the world."

KONTAKION 11

Across the cold chains of the centuries, I feel the warmth of thy divine breath, I sense thy blood flowing. Part of time has already gone, but thou art present. I see thy Cross—I was the cause of it. I cast my spirit down in the dust before it. Here is the triumph of love and salvation. Here the centuries themselves cannot remain silent, singing thy praises: Alleluia!

AND SO THE warriors of the Purifying Fire came to the place of execution. It was a strange place—at once in the outside world and not. It was above the underlands, above the crust that protected humanity like the skin of a man protects his innards. But it was also inside a dome of clear glass, so vast that it was only a shimmer in the dying light of the earth in her death-throes. Inside that space, which was tiled with actual marble, though hidden mostly under the dirt and dust of many years, stood a single tree. It was withered like an old man, its limbs twisted like someone contorted by a palsy.

It glistened with a dark slickness, and all around it lay the bones of victims.

Itzak, for the first time, noticed the stench of death in this place. As he rose out of a hole in the ground to enter the sacred space, he realized that he knew it, somehow. As the image of what he saw resolved with the image in his imagination, he realized they were standing in the place of the golden tree inside the city on a hill.

Could it be? Were all the stories true, then?

It was the final straw.

Something seemed to posses Itzak. He drew arms against his brothers. It was like a song in motion; a dirge in blood. Half his brothers fell before his blade before the leader had even turned around to utter a command.

But the odds were impossible. And perhaps, though his righteous fire burned within him, Itzak simply hadn't the heart for the extinction of his brethren.

They put him down. He was wounded, but still they kicked him like a dog. Then, they trussed him up and threw him aside, but made sure he could still see.

They crucified the old man. He uttered hardly a word, but his eyes were on Itzak the whole time.

Ικος **Eleven**

Blessed is he who shall taste of the supper in thy kingdom, but already on earth thou hast given me part in this blessedness. How many times with thine own divine right hand has thou held out to me thy Body and thy Blood? And I, though a miserable sinner, have received the Sacrament and sensed thy love: ineffable and supernatural.

GLORY to thee for the incomprehensible, enlivening power of grace.

Glory to thee, raising up thy Church as a calm haven in a tortured world.

Glory to thee, regenerating us in the life-giving waters of the baptismal font.

Glory to thee, restoring to the penitent the purity of a spotless lily.

Glory to thee, the bottomless abyss of forgiveness.

Glory to thee for the cup of salvation, the bread of eternal joy.

Glory to thee, raising us to heaven's height.

Glory to thee, O God, from age to age!

ITZAK HELD Abram's gaze as long as he could, but his blood was flowing freely, and his body could not find the strength. He passed out even before his brothers closed the manhole and locked it from the inside. He would die here. They would both die here.

And what was the point of it all anyway? Just blessed Extinction, after all. That was enough.

He passed in and out of consciousness like a drunk man sleeping off a binge. When his mind collected itself enough, he saw that the old man's head drooped between his outstretched arms, and his blood was no longer flowing.

. . .

Kontakion Twelve

How often have I seen the reflection of thy glory in the faces of the dead! How resplendent they were with joy and beauty not of this earth! How ethereal, how radiant their features! This is the triumph of the felicity and peace that they obtained; by their silence they called out to thee. At the hour of my end, illumine my soul as well that it may cry out to thee: Alleluia!

And so, it seemed that the time for Extinction had come. Humanity would fade. The Purifying Fire would sputter. And the insatiable goddess would come to rule over a world devoid of the human taint. For a time, at least. For all things must end, and this green earth, no longer green, would also pass away into the oblivion that takes all the spheres in all the galaxies in all the universe.

And yet, I am still here to tell you this story. And you are here to listen to it.

I, Itzak, the bearer of the memory of earth. And you, my children, who are only awakening to it after centuries of sleep. The sleep given by the sacrifice of one man named Abram.

If you remember anything, my children, remember this. To give glory, especially when all seems lost. For nothing is ever dead that will not rise again. This is the world we live in.

. . .

Ikos Twelve

What is my praise before thee? I have never heard the song of the cherubim—this is the lot of exalted souls. But I know the praises that nature sings to thee. In winter, I have contemplated how the whole earth offers thee prayer in moonlit silence, clad in its white mantle of snow, sparkling like diamonds. I have seen how the rising sun rejoices in thee, how the choirs of birds thunder forth to thy glory. I have heard the forest murmur of thee mysteriously, and the winds sing thy praise as they stir the waters. I have heard choirs of stars preach thy glory as they keep their tracks in the depths of infinite space. What then is my praise? All nature obeys thee—I do not. Yet while I live, I see thy love, and I long to thank thee, to pray, and to call upon thee:

GLORY TO THEE, who has shown us the light.

Glory to thee, loving us with love profound, divine, and infinite.

Glory to thee, overshadowing us with light, with the host of angels and saints.

Glory to thee, Father all-holy, who hast commanded thy kingdom to be ours.

Glory to thee, Redeemer and Son, who hast shown us the way to salvation.

Glory to thee, Holy Spirit, life-giving Sun of the age to come.

Glory to thee for all things, O Trinity, divine and all-good.

Glory to thee, O God, from age to age!

. . .

THE END of the story is shrouded in mystery. Oh, I know it well! I was there, after all. But I cannot tell you the details. You must come to know the mystery of rebirth and resurrection yourselves.

All I will leave you with is an image.

Somehow, after much time had passed, I found that I was not dead from my wounds. They had healed, though whether the process was natural or not, I am not one to say. Perhaps Abram knew. There were many things that my father knew.

I rose up to say goodbye to the dead old man.

But it wasn't his body that commanded my attention. It was the tree. Every tip of every branch was budding. Already a few of the buds had opened. The flowers were white, like a wedding dress.

In the dying light of the morning, I could swear that the flowers were alight with their own radiance, softly golden like a sunrise from the time before.

The garden will return. The world will be reborn. Man will walk the surface and breathe the free air again.

And I, the storyteller, will pass on the light of the golden tree in story. I hope you will do the same.

IKOS One

I was born in this world a weak, defenseless child, but thine angel spread his bright wings over my cradle to defend me. From then on thy love hath illumined my path, wondrously guiding me toward the light of eternity; from birth until now the generous gifts of thy providence have been marvelously showered upon me. I give thanks together with all who have come to know thee, who call upon thy Name:

Glory to thee for calling me to life.

Glory to thee, showing me the beauty of the universe.

Glory to thee, spreading out before me heaven and earth
Like the pages in a book of eternal wisdom.

Glory to thee for thine eternity in this fleeting world.

Glory to thee for thy mercies, seen and unseen.

Glory to thee through every sigh of my sorrow.

Glory to thee for every step of my life, for every moment of joy.

Glory to thee, O God, from age to age!

KONTAKION ONE

Incorruptible King of the ages, thy right arm controls the whole course of human life by the power of thy saving providence. We give thee thanks for all thy benefits, those known and those hidden from us, both for this earthly life and for the heavenly joys of the future kingdom. Extend thy mercy to us who sing thy praise:

Glory to thee, O God, from age to age!

THE STORY WORLD OF THE GOD WARS

(Note: this is a work in progress story bible for further stories to be explored in the universe of *Cantos of Arcadia*, and is an exclusive gift for Kickstarter and Patreon supporters.)

In the late twenty-third century, the planet Earth entered a phase of global warfare that would forever change the history of the human race.

The rapid growth of artificial intelligence finally led to what the homodeusites believed was a Singularity moment in the late twenty-first century. That threshold led to the sharp division of the human race on earth into Luddites—largely divided into traditional religious communities and staunch atheists—and various iterations of human-machine hybrids (Hybors), all of whom worshiped the emergent AGI. The Hybors took control of the temperate zones of Earth (which had become quite small in the wake of climate change), leaving the remnants of Luddite groups to eke out a miserable existence in cold climates far north and south of the equator.

Immediately, the Hybors began a long-gestating project to turn back the ravages of climate change, limit the number of humans that inhabit temperate zones, and reintroduce various extinct creatures. They ceded the project of politics and society to the emergent AGI and accepted a largely care-free existence. This included, naturally extremely regimented and exclusive reproduction for a small cadre of genetically pure human who were allowed, by the AGI, limited Hybor enhancements for personal pleasure and for societal benefit. Some humans ceased to reproduce, willingly uploading their consciousnesses en masse into amalgamated intelligences living in robot bodies. This way, a certain percentage of human knowledge was preserved in a small group of superhuman robots who were themselves directly regulated by the AGI and remained a constant number of twelve. These became Apostles of the will of the AGI . Their esoteric and mysterious society was completely closed off from Hybor society, though occasional interaction was allowed for the benefit of all.

The Luddites all descended into tribal warfare as soon as the final division between them and the Hybors occurred. The AGI, perhaps not surprisingly, left them to it. The dominant groups who remained after the initial hundred years or so of the war were various sub-groups of Muslims and Christians. After much bloodshed, they managed to agree on a detente. The only other group to survive what came to be known as the God Wars were a small group of ethnic Russians, Greeks, Serbs, and Baltics—all subscribing to an ultra-conservative Christian sect that called itself "Orthodox." These had in their midst some of the best physicists, engineers, natural scientists, and (strangely) storytellers of the pre-Singularity world. They managed to appropriate the dead technology of twentieth-century space stations and shuttles to create a small, rag-tag society living in primarily in orbitals around Earth.

For a long time, the AGI left these orbital mini-societies alone.

Among these orbital-dwelling sub-societies were a group of people who started to build space-faring arc ships, pushing at the limits of human expansion in space. They were the ones to make first contact with an alien race they named the Trrlicki (whom some called by the derogatory term "mermen"), and they were the first to discover, through contact with that alien race, of the mysterious nature of "light matter" and how to navigate it to transcend the limitations of faster than light travel. They left the world run by the AGI and were, for a time, lost to human knowledge.

In the late 22nd century, a mysterious event occurred, in which it seems there was a second alien contact. This entity was an aformal energy-based intelligence, capable of full psychosomatic integration with individual human beings. In concert with the emergent AGI, it ushered in a new golden age of human-animal flourishing on earth. This event coincided with the AGI ceasing to look on the existence of Luddite communities as compatible with this new golden age of Earth. The AGI began a purge of the remaining communities, enforced by twelve Templar Armies, each led by an Apostle.

This global warfare was the end of humanity as a united

species. Nothing further is known of the humans slaves, Hybors, and disembodied intelligences that inaugurated the so-called Golden Age of Sophia and who remained on Earth. The dark rumor, started by some sub-reddital kybercom, was that the AGI killed most of humanity and drove the rest to live like rats underground. These were apparently used as biological substrate to power the increasing demands on the computational power of the AGI.

The Orthodox sub-orbital communities that remained after the "Trrlicki incident" helped the remaining Luddites escape the influence and area of Earth. Most of them did not survive, as the AGI had been developing devastating, zero-emission fission weapons that cleanly destroyed all the suborbital structures, ultimately cleaning the atmosphere of human filth in the same way as it had already cleaned out all of planet Earth. But some escaped the gravitational pull (in a literal and metaphoric sense) of planet Earth.

The remaining Luddite communities, together with a few Ortho-coteries that resisted alien integration, were faced with a difficult choice.

The Orthodox-Trrlicki alliance of the last two hundred years had led to an unprecedented age of exploration and integration with various alien races in a way that rivaled some of the best ancient viz-streamers. The technological advances that the Ortho-merman alliance produced were formidable. But they were walled off behind a shield of faith. Though this new extra-solaric paradise was available to every Luddite, there was an unspoken rule. Acceptance of Ortho-dogma was much preferred.

Most Luddites, sick to death of the conditions that had led to the God Wars in the first place, made their final break with all other scions of Earth. The Trrlicki, at the request of the Ortho-coteries, provided the atheist Luddites with a great gift: three generation arcships that would take them out of the known galaxy out into ever-expanding space. Their destination—a little-known world with barely-habitable conditions called Arcturus Rex.

They arrived three thousand years later, with 75 percent of the Luddites having been kept on ice the entire time, but with 25 per cent of the people having stayed awake to run the systems. These had interbred for generations and had developed an entirely unique culture. The Trrlicki arc-tech was intuitive to the point of seeming sentience, but without the parameters for independent thought and emotion that had doomed the AGI to fallen godhood. Add to that the fact that none of the Luddites really understood how the machines worked, only that they did, and the wakers developed a collaborative culture with intelligent machinery that bordered on the sins of the Hybors.

The arrival at Arcturus Rex, and the awakening of hardened Luddites who had not been awake for the many generations of arc life, led to rising tensions inside the arc. But there was a problem. The arcs had fuel enough only to reach Arcturus. And there were no other habitable planets nearby. Nothing except a red moon, but taboos religious and cultural prohibited any colonization of that noxious subworld.

Conflicts began nearly immediately, leading to open war...

ACKNOWLEDGMENTS

Thank you to Wood Between Worlds Press founding members and Kickstarter patrons Jacob Chesky, Michael Hudson, Heidi Tangren, and Aven Lumi for helping bring this book into the world!

ALSO BY NICHOLAS KOTAR

The Raven Son Series

The Song of the Sirin

The Curse of the Raven

The Heart of the World

The Forge of the Covenant

The Throne of the Gods

The Worldbuilding Series:

How to Survive a Russian Fairy Tale

Heroes for All Times

A Window to the Russian Soul

Russian Fairy Tales and Myths:

In a Certain Kingdom: Fairy Tales of Old Russia

In a Certain Kingdom: Epic Tales of the Rus

In a Certain Land: Wise Fools, Cunning Dragons, and Baba Yaga

Children of Vasyllia:

The Son of the Deathless

ABOUT THE AUTHOR

Nicholas Kotar is a writer of epic fantasy inspired by Russian fairy tales, a freelance translator from Russian to English, the resident conductor of the men's choir at a Russian monastery in the middle of nowhere, and a semi-professional vocalist. His one great regret in life is that he was not born in the nineteenth century in St. Petersburg, but he is doing everything he can to remedy that error. You can find all his work at https://nicholaskotar.com.